D0145071

Evermore

Also from Corinne Michaels

The Salvation Series
Beloved
Beholden
Consolation
Conviction
Defenseless
Evermore – 1001 Dark Nights Novella
Indefinite (Coming 2019)

Return to Me Series
Say You'll Stay
Say You Want Me
Say I'm Yours
Say You Won't Let Go: A Return to Me/Masters and Mercenaries
Novella

Standalone Novels
We Own Tonight
One Last Time
Not Until You
If I Only Knew

Co-written Novels with Melanie Harlow
Hold You Close

Evermore

A Salvation Series Novella

By Corinne Michaels

1001 Dark Nights

EVIL EYE
CONCEPTS

Evermore
A Salvation Series Novella
By Corinne Michaels

1001 Dark Nights

Published by Evil Eye Concepts, Incorporated

Acknowledgments from the Author

If you endure any time with me during this process, you deserve so much more than a thank you that's back here. For real, I'm a little crazy and you know this, but...here it is.

To my husband and children. I don't know how you deal with me, but I can't tell you how much I appreciate you. I love you all with my whole heart.

My beta readers, Katie & Melissa: Thank you so much for your support and love during this book. I love you guys and couldn't imagine not having you.

My assistant, Christy Peckham: I would fire you, but you keep coming back so I'll just say thank you.

My readers. There's no way I can thank you enough. It still blows me away that you read my words. You guys are everything to me. Everything.

Bloggers: You're the heart and soul of this industry. Thank you for choosing to read my books and fit me into your insane schedules. I appreciate it more than you know.

Melanie Harlow, thank you for being the good witch in our duo or Ethel to my Lucy. Really you're the good witch and I'm the bad, but your friendship means the world to me and I love writing with you (especially when you let me kill characters).

Bait, Stabby, and Corinne Michaels Books — I love you more than you'll ever know.

My agent, Kimberly Brower, I am so happy to have you on my team. Thank you for your guidance and support.

Melissa Erickson, you're amazing. I love your face.

Vi, Claire, Mandi, Amy, Kristy, Penelope, Kyla, Rachel, Tijan, Alessandra, Syreeta, Meghan, Laurelin, Kristen, Kennedy, Ava, and Natasha—Thank you for keeping me striving to be better and loving me unconditionally.

Dedication

To the readers who have loved and nurtured this series. Thank you for always being my salvation!

One Thousand and One Dark Nights

Once upon a time, in the future…

*I was a student fascinated with stories and learning.
I studied philosophy, poetry, history, the occult, and
the art and science of love and magic. I had a vast
library at my father's home and collected thousands
of volumes of fantastic tales.*

*I learned all about ancient races and bygone
times. About myths and legends and dreams of all
people through the millennium. And the more I read
the stronger my imagination grew until I discovered
that I was able to travel into the stories… to actually
become part of them.*

*I wish I could say that I listened to my teacher
and respected my gift, as I ought to have. If I had, I
would not be telling you this tale now.
But I was foolhardy and confused, showing off
with bravery.*

*One afternoon, curious about the myth of the
Arabian Nights, I traveled back to ancient Persia to
see for myself if it was true that every day Shahryar
(Persian: شهريار, "king") married a new virgin, and then
sent yesterday's wife to be beheaded. It was written
and I had read, that by the time he met Scheherazade,
the vizier's daughter, he'd killed one thousand
women.*

Something went wrong with my efforts. I arrived in the midst of the story and somehow exchanged places with Scheherazade – a phenomena that had never occurred before and that still to this day, I cannot explain.

Now I am trapped in that ancient past. I have taken on Scheherazade's life and the only way I can protect myself and stay alive is to do what she did to protect herself and stay alive.

Every night the King calls for me and listens as I spin tales. And when the evening ends and dawn breaks, I stop at a point that leaves him breathless and yearning for more. And so the King spares my life for one more day, so that he might hear the rest of my dark tale.

As soon as I finish a story... I begin a new one... like the one that you, dear reader, have before you now.

Chapter One

Gretchen

"What do you mean you're not coming?" I scream into the receiver at my what-should-be husband.

"I can't marry you," Harold tells me.

My eyes fill with angry tears. "You decided this *now*?" I shriek.

It's my wedding day.

Well, it was supposed to be. Harold—which is the worst name in existence when you're in the throes of passion—apparently has decided it won't be.

An hour late, I might add. I'm here, at the church, in my nine-thousand-dollar wedding dress that I saved for. Without a groom.

I'm going to kill him.

My voice drops eerily soft. "Whatever the hell the issue is, we can deal with it tomorrow, Harold. You can't do this to me. You get your ass to this church and you marry me."

He sighs. "I can't do it. I can't, Gretchen. I had an epiphany last night."

An epiphany? How rich. "Was it that you're a dickhead who was going to destroy the woman who stood by you the last seven-fucking-years?"

"I'm saving you."

Now I've heard it all. "Saving me, my ass!" I scream. "You will not do this to me. You won't make me a jilted bride! I won't let you." My two best friends, Catherine and Ashton, share a look as they stand in their rose gold colored bridesmaids dresses.

Harold goes silent and then I hear someone in the back. "It's for the better. We never should've done this. You're my associate at the firm and if we do this, it will destroy both of our careers."

A tear falls down. I'm so angry. I'm so betrayed by him. Seven years we've been sneaking around. I was his "Secret Slut" as I called myself. At first it was exciting. The sneaking around, late-night office romps, the little touches we'd share knowing that later we wouldn't have to slow down.

Then it became impossible. I wanted to go to him when a case went bad, but I couldn't because he was my boss. Gossip in the office became much more than harmless chatter, so we pulled back even more.

Finally, two months ago, he'd had enough of me complaining and threatening to end things. He proposed and said he wanted to marry me immediately. That if we were married, I could take equal part in the firm and finally stop having to hide our relationship.

My chest rises and falls because now, there's no going back. People know. People are here to witness this, and now I'll be the "left-at-the-alter lawyer."

Fuck him.

"This is only better for you." My voice is loud, as I no longer have any control. "You are the only person this benefits, you tiny-dick bastard! You were supposed to marry me! You were supposed to finally take me out of the damn hole you threw me in when you slept with me seven years ago."

"Gretch?" Catherine asks softly and I glare at her. The three of us have been friends since grade school. She puts her hands in the air, knowing there's no way I can even remotely stop now. I'm livid.

Ashton giggles. "This is so going to be good."

"You suck as a lawyer!" I continue my tirade, deciding that it's time to let him know what a favor I was doing him all these years. "You suck as a lover! I faked an orgasm at least half the time and I hope your balls shrivel up. Oh," I huff. "One more thing, I quit and I hope you lose every damn case I was working on!"

I hang up the phone, throwing it across the room and shattering it into hundreds of pieces. Ashton gives a slow clap. "That...was impressive."

"Oh my God." I grip my throat. "Did I just quit my job?"

Catherine takes a step forward. "Yeah, babe."

There's a knock on the door and Jackson peeks his head in. "So, I tried to cover the yelling up with music, but..."

"Everyone heard," I finish.

He nods. "I'm sorry."

Jackson is a great man, even if he did make my best friend move across the damn country to California. She's happy. She loves him. And he adores her more than what should be humanly possible. As much as our friendships have changed, it doesn't matter the miles that separate us, our hearts are still close.

Although, I'm not quite sure I'll have a heart after this.

For an hour I stood here, waiting, thinking he was going to show up and it would be fine. For two months I've been waiting for today. For years I've had to hide the fact that as a senior associate I've been in a secret relationship with my boss. He was the one who said he wanted to marry me and be a real couple after our last fight.

Turns out he only wanted to shut me up.

My breathing starts to accelerate and I feel like the dress is trying to strangle me.

"It'll be okay." Catherine rubs my back. "You're going to be fine, just take a deep breath."

"I lost my fiancé and quit my job, I'm…I'm so screwed."

Ashton nods. "You are totally screwed, but you'll be okay."

Leave it to her to be an asshole. My eyes turn to her and I glower. "You need to work on your sympathy, Ash. I'm a lawyer and even I felt that."

"Yes, but you're a lawyer with a heart. Also, look who isn't hyperventilating anymore."

I flip her off.

"Ignore her," Catherine cuts in and then slaps Ashton's shoulder. "We'll handle everything. Jackson, please get her out the back. I'll take care of the guests."

Jackson wraps his jacket around my shoulders and tucks me into his side.

"I'm sorry, Gretchen, he's an idiot. I'm happy to beat the shit out of him if it would make you feel better."

I smile at his offer. "Thanks, but I'll pass for now."

We get to the car without anyone seeing me. Jackson tucks me into the back, kisses my cheek, and then heads in to help his wife deal with my family, who I can only imagine are losing their minds. They start to pour out, and I sit here with tears streaming, grateful the limo has blacked-out windows, that way, no one can see me fall apart. Mortified and husbandless.

Chapter Two

Gretchen

Unemployment doesn't suit me.

At all.

And it's only been seven days.

I got a call from Harold yesterday, telling me that he understood my reasons, but if I wanted to reconsider, I was welcome to come back. I told him to fuck off and lose my number.

Then he asked where my notes were.

I sent a photo of the ashes in my fireplace.

"I'm going to head back to California soon," Catherine says as she organizes the wedding present pile. She opened them all, cataloged them, and has offered to handle getting them sent back.

I think the least I should get is the airfryer, but she says no.

"Well, I'm now the proud recipient of two round-trip tickets to anywhere and a stay at one of their hotels. Once I'm homeless, I can fly out to you and live on your couch."

She looks up and rolls her eyes. "You're not going to be homeless, Gretch. You're far too organized for that. We all know you have a year's worth of income in reserve, plus it's not like you can't get another job."

I release a heavy sigh. "Not the point."

"No, that's exactly the point," Ashton, who refuses to leave, says as she enters the room with a bowl of popcorn. "You don't have to work. You can take some time, find the right firm, travel, send body parts in boxes to Harold for fun, do whatever you want."

"Body parts?"

She shrugs. "We're from Jersey…we know people."

I laugh. "I'll have you know that our families work in *legitimate* waste management companies."

Ashton smirks. "That's what they want us to think."

"My mother is so upset, she can't even eat," I say.

Ashton snorts. "I can't believe she didn't force Harold down the aisle claiming he ruined her daughter."

My mother is a nutjob and still believed I was a virgin and needed advice for my marriage night. That was until my cousin spit her wine across the table and blurted out that I've been banging my boss for years.

Mom has been unable to really speak to me since then. I'm going to hell and she can't bear witness.

"Well, don't be surprised when Harold goes missing because Uncle Salvatore is adding his house to his route. God only knows what that means."

I burst out laughing, imagining Ashton's uncle doing just that. He was very vocal after the what-should've-been-wedding how no one hurts his *familia*.

Jackson clears his throat. "And they say Navy SEALs are scary."

She pops a kernel in her mouth and raises a brow. "They've got nothing on Jersey girls."

"Speaking of Navy SEALs," I start. "Have you heard from Quinn?"

Now it's her turn to look uncomfortable. "No. When he's gearing up to deploy, I never do."

"We all deal with them differently—" Jackson starts to say but Catherine places her hand on his arm.

"Don't you dare defend him. Her claws will come out and we'll have to surgically remove them from your chest," Cat warns.

Ashton has been dating Quinn for over a year, if you can call it that. I don't even know what they're doing, but once again, she's pissed at him. I think of her like a feral cat. She looks cute from a distance but when you get close—she bites.

"My point is"–Ashton speaks as though none of that just happened—"that you can do whatever the hell you want. You don't have to stay here and look for a job. Maybe getting away would be good.

You know, cleanse the soul and also have an alibi when he turns up in the Hudson."

"That would be great if I didn't sell my condo and again—homeless."

We were supposed to move into Harold's place in a month. My condo is—was—the best location and I loved it here. Now, I have nothing.

"You're more than welcome in California."

As much as I would love to spend time with Catherine and Jackson, I need to work. I can't be lying around on their couch, plus, they've only been married about six months. The last thing I really want to do is listen to them all sweet and honeymoon-like every night.

I was supposed to be on my honeymoon.

Instead, I cashed that shit in before he could and I got airline tickets and a hotel for down the line.

He left me at the altar, least I can get is a trip.

"I appreciate that, I really do, but I'm already freaking behind because of him." I release a groan that almost sounds like a cry. "I'm never going to have kids now and I can forget my career goals! I need to find a new job. My life list requires that I don't have a lot of time to lose."

I've been a workaholic my entire life, I can't imagine having an extended time off.

"Oh here we fucking go," Ashton mutters while rolling her eyes.

"What?"

"The life list. Number one, be married and have the perfect life. Number two, stab Gretchen in the eye with her stupid list. Number three, burn the list and remind Gretchen that living isn't a science."

"Ash." Catherine tries to mollify her. "You and I think the list is…extreme, but Gretchen likes it."

"Yes. I do. I need lists to keep things in order. Besides, my mother always said a dream isn't a plan until it's written down."

There's nothing wrong with keeping things in order. I feel like having a life list has ensured that most of my plans, though not all, have worked out the way they should.

Sure, all the things that I believed I could check off on my list have now gone to shit, but at one point, they almost came true.

"Oh God!" I say with tears in my eyes.

"What?" Catherine rushes over. "Are you okay?"

I look at my best friend and shake my head. "He ruined everything! My entire life list is now gone! *None* of it is even possible. There's no way I'll even have kid number one by the time number two was due!"

I had a great job, that's gone. I was getting married, that's not happening. I was in my dream condo, which I can't afford to keep now even if I did pull the sale. Everything all because of stupid Harold.

"Then it's time for a new list." Cat takes my hand. "Life is about adapting and now it's time to do that."

"I hate him."

"As you should," she agrees.

Ashton sighs. "Body parts in a box anyone?"

I let out a giggle and wipe the tears. I have the best friends. Catherine cancelled her trip back to California to see me through this. Ashton called out of work, and Jackson has...well, offered his services. I know it all feels so bleak right now, but with them on my side, I'll be okay.

"My offer still stands to break his kneecaps," Jackson attempts again.

"Now that I may change my mind about."

He laughs. "I do have another option if you're open to hearing me out."

"Really?"

Now I'm intrigued.

He nods. "First, how do you feel about moving to Virginia Beach?"

* * * *

"I can't believe you're leaving me, too!" Ashton bitches as she helps me pack another box. "First Cat, now you?"

I can't believe I'm moving either. I never imagined I would be going to work for Jackson. I'm not exactly an expert on anything military, but he swears there's a case that he could really use my help with.

I'm pretty sure it's a pity position, but right now, I'll take it.

Not only do I get to get the hell out of here, but I'll be surrounded by hot guys with guns. This might just be the best job ever.

"You spend half your time in Virginia Beach when Quinn is

around," I counter.

"Yeah, but he's gone and I spend that time with you."

"I'll miss you too, Ash, but I need this."

She shrugs. "I know. Doesn't mean I won't miss you. And since you said yes to the job offer you seem...lighter."

I feel lighter. It's been almost as if just making the decision took some of the weight off. The part that isn't fun is leaving Ashton. We've been the two of us since Cat left for California a few years ago. I'm going to miss her.

I pull my tough exterior, mush on the inside friend into my arms. I am sad to be leaving. I love where I live, the food, my family and friends. But I can't stay. Everything right now reminds me of Harold and that's when the light feeling I'm enjoying starts to crash.

"Maybe you can come down there? There are IVF clinics that I'm sure would love to have you."

Ashton is what I call a miracle worker. Her success rate is impressive, and her humility about it even more so. She's not exactly the humblest person regarding anything—except her job. To her, it's not about the numbers, it's about the parents who are trying so hard for their babies. Being an embryologist has been her true calling in life.

Sometimes I'm reminded that her black heart isn't really so black.

"I won't go anywhere near Virginia Beach until Quinn Miller gets his stupid, thick, ridiculous head out of his ass. I'm not giving him the slightest hope that we'll get back together."

"Yeah. Okay."

"What?" she scoffs.

I know she wants to talk a good game, but she loves him. Always has—since she met him—and always will.

"Nothing. I just think you and Quinn complement each other."

"By both being stubborn?"

"Pretty much. You both love each other, no matter what you're hellbent on showing."

"I don't love him. I don't even like him. I want a future, a life, a family and he wants...who the fuck knows!"

If she didn't care, none of this would bother her, but I won't point that out because I'd like our goodbye not to be her hating me.

"Well, I get it. Also, I'm probably the last person who should be giving love advice."

"Love is for suckers."

I laugh. "Love can suck it."

"Love is a dumb bitch."

"Love is a lying whore."

Ashton nods. "Love is pathetic and mean."

"Love really hurts when you lose it."

Her phone starts to buzz, but she ignores it, caught up in our declarations of what love can do.

"Love can go right to hell with the dumb men who hurt women like us."

"You going to grab that?" I ask as the vibrating sound starts up again.

Ashton grabs her phone and plops on the couch. "Hey, Cat." She uses the excuse to stop packing, which really wasn't happening anyway, but now it's definitely not. "I'm at Gretchen's. Yeah, she's here, I mean, I'm not here alone." She pauses and then sighs. "I'm helping."

"Helping," I snort. She's done barely anything.

"Yes, Mom. I'll give her the phone. Here." Ashton hands me the phone.

"Hey, what's up?"

"So," Catherine says with a hint of excitement in her voice. "I'm here at the office with Jackson, checking on things before we fly out."

"Right."

"Gretch, do you remember Benjamin Pryce?"

Now that's a name I haven't heard in forever.

A shiver runs down my spine as a perfect image of his face comes to mind.

"Gretchen?" Catherine calls my name when I don't say anything.

"Yeah, of course. I don't think I ever could forget him. He was my first kiss."

And my first love.

Every woman knows, and remembers, her first kiss. We were those friends who made a pact that by seventh grade, if we hadn't been kissed, we'd kiss each other.

Sure enough, my super nerd vibe wasn't exactly bringing me a slew of boys that wanted to kiss me. So Ben did.

It was sweet.

And awkward.

And braces were totally not sexy, but Ben was my friend and a nerd like me. He told me after that he watched a ton of movies to try to get it right. I smiled, loving that he cared. It was that moment that I realized just how much I loved him.

"He was your first kiss? How did I not know that?"

"No idea. Anyway, I haven't forgotten him, why are you asking?"

"So, I was taking a call, not paying attention, and this guy walks into Jackson's office...I knew I recognized him, but I couldn't place it. Then he remembered me. But my point is, dude, Ben has really grown up."

"Wait, he's there?" I ask. "At Cole Securities?"

"Yup, yup he is." Catherine's voice drops. "He has...umm...transformed. He's very different than what you remember."

I shake my head. "Okay? What does that even mean?"

"I'm just saying, you have a friend here! One who specifically asked about you too."

He asked about me? That seems so weird. I haven't heard from him since he left after I told him I was in love with him. He promised to stay in touch, and then he was gone. I figured he just forgot about me or at least wanted to forget, which is why he disappeared. He was the first boy I ever loved and it broke my heart when I never heard from him again.

"Okay, but...it's not like that. We're not friends anymore. Once upon a million years ago we were..."

"No, but there's nothing saying old flames can't be rekindled! Just wear something cute. Trust me. That pink dress or even the blue." There's a weird tone she's using. I don't like it.

"Catherine?"

"I have to go. I'll see you tomorrow when you get here! Love you!"

I look down at the phone and then back to Ashton. "Well, that was weird."

She laughs. "Catherine is weird. What did she say?"

"Apparently Ben, from middle school, is working for Jackson."

Ashton purses her lips and taps her nails on the arm of the chair. "Ben?"

"The guy I was friends with who moved away in high school...the one I told you about that I really liked and kept waiting to call me."

"Not ringing any bells."

She wouldn't remember him anyway, he definitely wasn't running in her crowd.

Ben was bullied, and his parents moved after it got really bad. But that isn't what has my heart pounding right now. I loved Ben. I really loved him and it took me almost all of high school to get over him. I waited for his letters, for him to come back to me like he promised. I thought if I loved him so much, that he could feel it wherever he was.

I was stupid.

I've always wondered if he was okay...I guess I'll find out soon enough.

Chapter Three

Gretchen

"Natalie!" I smile with my arms open as I walk toward her.

I love this girl. She's funny, smart, sweet as can be, and despite having a shit sandwich handed to her, she smiles a lot. Then again, if I got to look at her husband all day, I'd smile too.

"Ahh!" She squeals as she gets out of her chair. "I heard you were coming to join this...group of idiots. I'm so glad you're here."

"Me too, I needed it. How are you? How is Liam and the kids?"

"They're good, you'll have to come by and see them."

"Once I get settled, I'd love that. For now, I'm just trying to get a hold on my life and new job here."

She touches my arm. "We're happy to have you. Mark needs all the help he can get. Plus, another girl in the office of testosterone will be much welcomed."

"How is our favorite minister?"

Mark Dixon is one of the best people on the planet and got himself ordained over the internet. He continues to claim he's a man of the cloth and we go with it because it's easier. He's insane. Basically, he's the penis-attached version of Ashton. They're both sarcastic and he'll keep me feeling like I'm home.

"He's fine. I love his wife, Charlie, and she beats him up when he acts like an ass—which means every day."

"She really is the best. I met her at Catherine's wedding and we talked a lot."

"Oh! I forgot about that. She's the best. Truly. She's probably the only woman alive who could deal with that man."

We both giggle.

"If it isn't Jilted."

Speak of the devil and he shall appear.

"You are not going to call me that, asshat."

"Oh, now that I know it bothers you, I totally am."

Great. It's like giving a dog a bone with these guys.

"Whatever you say, Twinkle Toes or was it Teeny Peenie? I can never remember your call sign."

His eyes widen and Natalie bursts out laughing.

"I can kill you, remember that," Mark warns.

"You could try, but your wife likes me and she'd kill you."

He grumbles about women under his breath.

Natalie claps her hands. "God, this is going to be the best place to work again."

For the first time since the wedding, I feel like I can breathe. My lungs don't hurt and there's not this dull pain in my chest. The issue is that I'm not sure if I'm more upset that Harold and I are over or that I lost my job.

"All kidding aside." I smile and put my professional face forward. "I'm really happy to be here. Whatever I can do to help, I'm up for the challenge."

"Mark," a deep, throaty voice says from behind me. "I have the next—"

I turn, and he stops.

Everything stops.

The world. My breathing. My heart. Time.

It just...dissipates.

I'm at a total loss for words because this man is gorgeous. He's at least six-foot-four with huge arms and a broad chest. There's a dark stubble on his face that makes him look both scary and yet trustworthy. The most important feature on a man, in my opinion, is his hands. This man has perfect hands.

But there, underneath the ridiculously sexy body, are eyes I remember. Ones that seem to know me too.

"Gretchen?"

Well, Ben has grown up and...wow. "Ben?"

He smiles and that boyish look is still the same. "Catherine said you were coming down to work here, but she didn't mention..."

"Mention what?"

He shakes his head and scratches the back of his neck.

I know my best friend failed to mention that he is sex on a stick and I shouldn't just dress cute, I should've dressed for any possibility of seeing GI Joe on crack.

"Didn't mention you'd be working together on the client Ben is heading?" Mark finishes. "Or that you'd want to undress her six ways till Sunday when you saw her?"

Natalie slaps his chest. "Really, Mark? Idiot." She steps forward. "Gretchen, I'll show you to the office you'll be working out of."

Ben puts his hand up. "I'll show her. No need to have you do it, Lee."

My heart accelerates a bit. Totally just nerves. Yup. Nerves.

"You're such a good guy, Ben. Unlike the other tools!" Natalie yells and they all grunt or groan. "Don't let any of these boys get an inch with you, got it?"

I've worked with men before, but I have a feeling this is a little different caliber of *men*. "I won't. Thank you. Maybe we can do lunch?"

She nods. "I'd love that."

Ben turns and I take my cue. We walk down the hall in silence, and then I clear my throat. "So, a SEAL?"

"I did my time in college, hated wearing a suit, and one of my buddies said he was joining the Navy. One thing led to another and I was following him right into my first commission."

"Wow."

"Yeah." He cracks his neck. "I figured if I was going to join, might as well try it all."

"How long were you in?" I ask as we stop in front of the door.

"Not as long as I would've liked."

I crinkle my eyes, confused because if he wanted to stay in, why didn't he?

"Well, thank you for your service."

Ben smirks with a laugh. "If you say that to everyone who served in this area, you'll lose your voice."

I nudge him with my arm. "Still, thank you. If I lose my voice, that's the least I can do to show my appreciation."

"Well, thank you for thanking me."

"I think you're missing the point of the thank you."

"I guess I am." Ben shrugs. "Tell me about your job..."

The first thing that comes to mind is my ex. My disgust rises as I think of him. Stupid asshole. But then comes disappointment, not because he's my ex, but because I love practicing law. I enjoyed researching, making lists, checking things off knowing that rules would work themselves out because of the laws people before me determined to be just.

Never in college did I think some man would be what I thought of first.

"Hmm..." I say the word slowly. "I was a contracts and litigation attorney. It's truly as fascinating as it sounds. Lots of reading, studying, reading over old cases and then coming up with a plan."

"Oh, I remember how much you love plans."

"I do." I smile.

"I would bet that you still keep lists for everything too..."

"You would be correct."

Ben shakes his head and I remember how much he thought I was a headcase for them. "I'm glad that some things haven't changed."

There's a look in his eyes that makes my heart race.

"Well, unlike you." I tuck my hair behind my ear, feeling really uncomfortable and shy. "You changed a lot."

He nods. "That I have."

"Not too much, though. You still have that mischievous look about you."

Ben chuckles. "Here we are."

He opens the door and I'm not sure what I was expecting, but it's more of a conference room than an office. There are two small desks and then a round table in the middle. I didn't think I'd have a corner office, but I wasn't really thinking I would share either. It's cozy, though, and for Jackson, hopefully I can help.

"Is there someone else that will be in here?" I ask.

"Yes. Me."

Well, shit.

"I see."

"We're sharing this office for now. Jackson thought since most of the work will require us both to bounce the info, no point in us having to walk back and forth. My office is usually right down the hall, but it's too small for another desk."

"Sounds very..." Stupid. Close. Intimate. Dumb. "...efficient."

He chuckles once. "Yeah. Good word."

"I'll take the left side if that's okay?"

"Sure. I don't really have a preference so whatever works." I put my purse down, grab a note pad and pen. "So what is the client you're working on and what do you need my legal knowledge for?"

Ben makes his way to the table, putting a bunch of folders together. "It's a foreign dignitary and his family. The dignitary is one thing, but his son is an...idiot. A total fucking moron. He keeps screwing up, getting his father into trouble, and we really needed a lawyer on payroll to help us when he screws up again."

"What has he done?"

"What hasn't he done? The issue isn't even the crap he pulls, it's what he hasn't gotten caught doing."

Makes me think of Ashton when we were kids. My mother didn't worry about what we were caught doing, it was the things we got away with. "Is there something he's into now? Some reason Jackson was urgent about me coming right away?"

Ben rubs his hand down his face. "Seventy-two hours ago, he disappeared."

"As in missing?"

Ben nods.

Jesus. What the hell kind of shit pile did I just willingly walk into? I've always known what Jackson does is dangerous. The man was shot, for Christsake. Then of course Aaron died—ish. Mark was kidnapped—then found.

This pep talk is really not helping.

I take a few cleansing breaths to slow my nerves. I'm not going to be in danger, I'm just here for legal help.

The key to crisis management is being level-headed. Which is what I will be.

"Have you alerted the authorities?" I ask.

"No. We can't."

"*What?*"

"We can't. We're operating *as* the authorities."

"Well then," I huff. "Why aren't you all out there looking for him? Why are you here with me?"

"I would love nothing more than to be out there doing something instead of being stuck in this office, but life doesn't give us what we want. I would only hinder the operation, furthering Cole Securities to be held liable for this fucking mess."

"I'm confused."

He pulls his pant leg up, showing me his prosthetic. "IED. So, here I am. Sidelined."

Chapter Four

Ben

That look. The one that reminds me that the life I dreamed of is fucking dead. The shock that then always turns to sadness for being a broken man.

I mourned it a long time ago, but I watch it every time someone else does.

If I have to see her do it, it'll be different.

Gretchen was that girl. The one I prayed would see we could be more than friends, and then, when we finally had our chance, I moved.

My father's job had us go from New Jersey to Idaho and he took it because of how badly I was picked on. I hated it. I hated leaving her. I would've taken an ass-kicking every day if it meant that I could be with her.

Sure, we were teenagers and it probably would've never worked, but there was something there and then I had to bury it. When I saw her again, it came rising to the top.

"Okay, then," Gretchen says a second later, her blonde hair falling in her face a little. "Let's do what we can from here. I figure we can use good old detective work and brain power. I've never really dealt with a kidnapping in litigation, but I'm sure there's something I watch on *CSI* that could come in handy, right?"

I'm stunned slightly. No questions? No millions of options that she thinks I should do? Where is the pity? Where's the sadness at the shattered dreams?

I wait for it, because it always comes.

I'm not sad nor do I feel bad for myself. I'm pissed, sure. I have regrets to some extent, but I'm lucky. I'm alive. Some of my friends weren't quite so lucky.

Immediately, I realize my mistake. I went there.

My mind fills with visions of the mission where we were riding in the Humvee, laughing, talking about TJ's fiancée and all the money that wedding was going to cost—and then suddenly, we weren't.

"Hey, Ben, you with me?" she asks, breaking me from my thoughts.

I shake my head. "You don't want to ask a million questions?"

"Well, I just asked one. If you could answer that, it would be great."

"I mean about my injury."

She shrugs. "Do you want to answer a million questions?"

"No."

"That's what I figured. If you want to tell me or talk, I'm here, but I know what it feels like to have people ask the same shit over and over again."

I remember what Catherine said about her being stood up, and nod. I can imagine that she's dealing with a lot, including people wanting to know information she probably doesn't even have.

But still, I'm not used to the reaction she gives. Almost like it doesn't matter.

"Still..." I say.

Her hand touches my arm. "I'm sorry you went through that. I really am. I know this is going to sound stupid or whatever, but I missed you, Ben. You were my best friend and I'm just really happy you're alive and here. I'm glad that right now, we're sitting in the same room and can talk. I really am."

"You missed me huh?" I nudge her.

"Well, I missed the scrawny kid who used to take the candy out of my bookbag when he didn't think I was looking. Who talked to me about how inaccurate movie scenes were based on random facts you knew. Not sure about The Hulk who is ridiculously hot, broody, with muscles...who is in front of me...and I'm going to shut up..." Gretchen seems to catch herself and her face turns bright red.

"Please. Do keep going..."

Gretchen was always gorgeous to me. I crushed on her all through school. She was the first girl I really had feelings for and when I left her, I hated my father. I had this adolescent dream that we would somehow be together. If she could just see...

Seems her eyesight is finally working.

"Anyway. The case. The missing kid, let's talk about that, and not your jacked-up body, okay?"

I decide to let her off the hook—for now.

"Sure, why don't we start at the beginning?"

She nods and sits beside me, taking a sheet of paper, and starts to read it. Instead of doing the same, I watch her. She's different and yet still in some ways, she hasn't changed at all. Her hair is much blonder, her eyes are still that aqua blue, though. I note the scar right under her eye from when she fell as we were playing tag. It's faded, but still there.

I wondered about her through the years. I hoped that she was okay. I've never been much for technology, plus we're not exactly encouraged to have a presence online, so I couldn't look her up.

But she's right here. Looking as beautiful as ever.

"How have you been? Truly, are you okay?" I ask, unable to stop myself, mostly because I just want more of an excuse to keep looking at her.

She shrugs. "I'm functioning."

"That sounds really encouraging." I laugh once.

"I'm sure you know that I'm here because I was left at the altar. I lost my job...well, I quit because I was sleeping with my boss who decided on my wedding day he didn't want to marry me. I was set to make partner at said job, so there's that. My life list has gone to total shit, and I was given a pity job from my best friend's husband. I mean, I'm really winning at life." Gretchen releases a heavy sigh and then covers her face. "Oh my God, I'm a mess."

I pull her hands down, hating that she felt the need to hide. "You're not a mess."

Her eyes go wide. "Did you not hear my life just now?"

"I did, but I bet I can do you one better," I challenge.

"Please. By all means."

She has no idea what she just asked for. I'm the poster child for mess. "I'm divorced because my wife couldn't handle the fact that I was injured. I lost my dream job, where I was literally kicking ass—daily. My parents passed away a year ago in a car wreck—while I was deployed. I live in a tiny ass apartment, after mooching off Jackson and Catherine because I basically shut myself down after my injury. I work here because Jackson and Mark won't let me quit, no matter how many times I've tried. Oh, and I literally lost an appendage."

"No fair." Gretchen glares.

"No, it's not."

She shakes her head. "No, you can't use the war injury as one of your life being a mess things. I call bullshit on that."

"Excuse me?"

Gretchen leans back in her seat with her arms over her very ample chest. "That's like the trump card that you can't play. Your wife leaving you, fine. Your job, I get. Even the housing thing, I'm totally with you on, because I too am now homeless and living in my best friend's husband, now boss's house. But you can't use your leg as a sucking point. Because it sucks, but it doesn't make you a mess."

I'm dying to hear her reasoning on that. "And how exactly does it not?"

"Because you, Benjamin Pryce, are a hero. A man who fought during a war and you survived. That's not a mess, my friend. Not even a little. Find another reason."

I laugh, a true, deep, hearty laugh for the first time in forever. She just called my ass out and doesn't look the least bit upset by it. As if all these years haven't passed and she's still the dorky kid's friend.

"You got balls, I'll tell you that," I toss back.

"Why, because your half-assed attempt at making your story sound worse didn't work?"

I think back to reasons and the one sticks out. Her life list. She still has that damn thing? I remember she would write, scratch out, write more, cross it off, and add again all throughout school. She felt that if she wrote it down, she put it out for the world to find.

I always thought she was ridiculous with it, but she swore it would work.

"Where the hell is your life list?"

"I don't want to talk about it."

Now it's my turn to grin. "Not a chance. You called me out, time to face the firing squad. Give it to me."

"No."

"Yes."

"No, I'm not giving it to you." Gretchen looks away but I see the glimpse of her smile.

"So you *do* have it? I bet it's even on you right now."

Her eyes narrow and she points a finger at me. "You will never see it."

I lean in, pulling her hand down and my lips turn up. "We'll just have to see about that."

Chapter Five

Gretchen

He smells so damn good, and arguing with him felt so natural. It was like all the years never passed and we're still the same people in some ways. Ben was the first person to really know me. He also never stopped making fun of my lists.

Lists are good.

They're a loose plan that keeps things on track.

Of course my life list could be burned at this point because none of it is working out right.

I look at my coat sitting on the chair, the pocket that's currently holding the list. I carry it with me everywhere. If I ever need to edit, it's always with me.

Suddenly, Ben's hands reach for the coat.

"Shit!" I yell but he already has it out.

"*Get married by thirty-three.*" He turns to me with a raised brow. "You missed that one."

"It's a fluid list. The timeline isn't the point, it's the goals."

I want to crawl in a hole right now.

He rolls his eyes and goes back to it. "*Make partner by thirty-five. Have first child by thirty-six.*" He grins. "I figured this would've been swapped that you'd want the kid before partner."

My eyes narrow. "Could you do this without the commentary?"

"Not likely."

"Of course not."

"*Second child within two years. Fit back in pre-pregnancy jeans three months after that.*" Ben's eyes meet mine. "Really? You're worried about your jeans enough to put it on your list?"

"Don't judge me."

"I'm just saying that your ass will look good no matter what."

I try not to blush. "Oh, well, thanks."

"Welcome."

"Give me the list back."

He smiles. "I'm not done yet."

"I hate you."

Ben's eyes return to the paper. "*Try a federal case and make headlines and rule the world.*" He reads aloud and my cheeks burn.

I forgot about the rule the world part. The rest is all accurate. Except that now none of that will actually happen. I snatch the list from his hand. "Jerkface."

"Gretch, you can't really think that living your life by some list is going to be what makes you happy."

"Yes, I can. If it all worked out, I would've been on track. I would've followed the plan, albeit a little delayed, but the list is the list."

"That's not happy," he says with his brown eyes piercing through me.

Happiness isn't what I take stock in. I don't need to be happy. I need order and for things to work the right way.

"It's what made sense."

"Plans are just that...a plan. They're not gospel and they sure as hell don't account for detours. You can't tell me that you wanted to have your plan met and your heart neglected."

No, can't say that it's what I wanted, but that's exactly what I was going to do.

Ben is so close, our bodies having somehow inched closer and closer. Our breaths mingle as we continue to speak, pull toward each other without even meaning to.

A knock on the door causes me to jump. Natalie is standing there with a shit eating grin on her face. "Sorry to interrupt, but there's a call you should take, Ben."

"I'll be right back and we'll finish this."

"Famous last words," I say under my breath as he walks out. That was what he told me the night he left after I told him I thought I loved him.

* * * *

Day three at Cole Securities has proven to be interesting. Ben hasn't been back in the office we're sharing since that first day. I've seen him in passing a few times, but he's on that phone constantly. I'm going to assume it's about the case, but no one is really saying much.

I've learned that they are very tight lipped and very serious. Which is fine by me, but I'm bored as hell. Instead of waiting around for someone to tell me what to do, I took it upon myself to start doing my own research on this kid. Well, he's not really a kid but whatever.

Thomas McEvoy was born December 23, 1996. He's spent most of his life traveling with his parents, being tossed from tutor to tutor. No real sense of a home because he's on number twelve.

He's done two stints in rehab and now has basically vanished.

Thomas is smart, rich, and has no sense of responsibility. He's lived his life doing whatever he wants without consequence.

After I learned whatever I could about him, I moved on to his father, Michael. He's a whole other set of concerns. The amount of money he's paying Cole Securities is a little insane, considering his country also has supplied security.

I mean, how many people are trying to kill you that you need an army surrounding you?

Now that I know what I can about the people, I need to figure out what exactly I can learn about how this connects to Jackson and this company. I start to review the contract. I'm not sure what exactly it is that Jackson needs me to decipher on a legal standpoint, but I figure that is going to come up at some point.

At first glance I would think it's a pretty standard contract. It has all the necessary loopholes to keep Cole Security out of any major litigation, but there's this one clause and I'm not sure how to interpret it.

My eyes read the words again, trying to see it in a new light.

"Anything interesting?" Ben's deep voice causes me to jump and fall out of my chair.

"Holy shit!" I say as my ass hits the floor.

"You all right?"

"I would've been if you'd made a noise."

Ben chuckles. "I was trained not to."

"Well, they did a good job," I note as I push myself up.

"You're jumpy."

"No, I just have been working alone the last few days and didn't expect to have someone sneak up on me."

His hand wraps around my arm, helping me to my feet. My body feels as though it's been zapped. Each muscle tightens and my skin tingles from where his skin is against mine. I can't explain it because it makes no sense, but it happens.

This man who I haven't seen in forever shouldn't be making my pulse spike. I should be completely unaffected, especially since it's been days without a word, but my stomach is in knots as I stare into his brown eyes.

"So..." He clears his throat.

"Right."

"The...umm..." Ben struggles.

"The contract," I finish. "I was looking over the contract and there's something..."

"Yes, the contract. What did you find?"

This is so awkward.

I move across to the other side of the table, needing a little distance because I'm not sure what to make of the moment we just had. This is my job. My only job and I can't be stupid. Jackson is relying on me and I won't let him down. If only I knew what the hell I was really doing here it might make this a little easier, but whatever.

I'm always up for a challenge.

Ben looks at the stacks of papers and I start to explain what I found.

"But this line..." I point to it. "It's not really bad per se, but I keep going back to it."

He reads it and scrunches his brows. "Whatever the hell that means."

I smile and then read it aloud in simple terms. "Basically they're saying that any form of gross negligence, willful neglect or misconduct that results in death or capture can be held against the company. In other words, they can sue if they feel Cole Securities wasn't doing it to their standards. Why would the company sign it?"

I would never allow this. One because those terms are too ambiguous. Two they're very hard to prove. And three, it leaves the company open to a lawsuit which the contract should be shooting to negate.

"That's not my department," Ben says while scratching his head. "I get the contracts once they're done."

"Do you know who would've prepared this contract?"

He shakes his head. "No, but Natalie would."

"Okay. I know there were some issues before within the company with a former employee or something, right?"

Catherine has always been tight-lipped regarding what happened. Which I respect. But now I feel like there's something missing.

"You should talk to Mark about that," Ben says. "I just know there was a lawyer on staff and he's not anymore."

"Okay, I'll do that today." It makes sense now why Jackson wanted me down here so quickly.

"What else did you find?"

We go over the piles more in depth. There was one other thing about his father, Michael that left me feeling confused. I show him the two pieces of information that were buried deep. Cole Securities does extensive background checks on their clients. I pull out the paper where there's a handwritten note.

"Okay, this part." I point. "He's a dignitary with diplomatic immunity, why hire a bunch of former SEALs? Why Jackson's company? He's been through four different high-level security companies in two years. It's weird, right? And then this..." I skim to find the line. "I'm not sure who did this report, but he mentions here something about a red flag regarding a financial discrepancy."

He almost has this look of pride at my discovery.

Ben nods his head once. "It's definitely something we should look at."

"Good."

At least my time wasn't wasted. I move my hand toward the other pile and Ben goes to it at the same time.

"Sorry," he says.

I start to open my mouth, but he speaks before I can.

"For sort of disappearing the last few days. There was a lead on Thomas's whereabouts and I had to follow it."

"It's fine, Ben."

"No, I should've come and told you. I was just so sure I had him and then it was a dead end."

It has to be frustrating for him. I can see the desire to *do* and yet he's stuck here. "It's really no big deal. I was plenty busy going through these things."

"You did a great job. I never would've looked at it from these angles," Ben compliments me and my heart flutters.

I'm ridiculous. There's no reason for my heart, or any other part of my body, to care about Ben.

"I'm just happy to help."

"We are too. We're a team around here and I'm glad you're on it."

I can count on one hand how many compliments I've heard in the last seven years. Harold didn't believe in compliments. He believed in results.

"You're making me blush," I tell him as I tuck the hair behind my ear.

His finger touches my chin, pulling it toward him. "You shouldn't hide, you're too beautiful when you're unguarded."

My head starts to spin and I don't know what to say. It's crazy that I'm feeling this way. It must be that I'm tired. Or hungry. Or maybe I'm just going through some post left-at-the-altar type breakdown.

Ben smiles. "I've really missed you, Gretchen."

"I really missed you, too."

I mentally slap myself for saying that. Definitely some breakdown. Now I just need it to stop.

Chapter Six

Gretchen

"I can't quit thinking about your list," Ben tells me as he takes a huge bite of his sandwich.

Not back to this again. It's been a week and each day he somehow brings up my stupid life plan that didn't work out. "Let's forget about my list."

"Why?"

Because the list is clearly not happening. Because my life isn't going to plan, unless the plan was to epically fail. Because everything on that list stemmed from me walking down the aisle that I never went down. *Pick a reason.*

Instead of admitting any of that, I just shrug. "No point."

"I disagree."

"You would because you're a man." A very big, hulky, sexy man who I've fallen asleep thinking of each night.

"You know what's funny?" he asks but doesn't give me the chance to answer. "That after all this time, it's the same with us. No awkwardness. No weird silence issues, it's just—normal."

"Because you're not normal," I say with a smirk.

"No denying that."

"You are different though. You're a lot bigger and scarier."

Ben leans in. "You don't seem scared."

Oh, I'm totally scared. Especially regarding the way my body reacts and the fact that I really want to know what his lips feel like against mine.

"You may be The Hulk, but I don't think you'll smash me."

He rolls his eyes. "I fucking hate that call sign."

Mark was all too happy to call him it a few times. I love the idea of call signs and that everyone eventually gets one in this crew. I thought we got to pick them, turns out that's not the case.

They're given.

And usually it's because you've done something stupid that they plan to use against you—forever.

"I need the story," I tell him as I pop a chip in my mouth.

"Not a fucking chance."

"I'll just ask Lee or Mark."

Ben grumbles. "Fine. I'll tell you. I busted a chair."

My hand pauses before the next chip enters. "You what?"

"I sat down, like a normal person, and the wooden chair busted."

I laugh once and then the look in his eyes makes me stop, but when he turns his head, I can't hold back. "You broke the chair?"

He groans while wiping his hand down his face. "Yes. It was clearly tampered with before I sat. I've sat in plenty of chairs without them breaking like that."

I collect my giggles seeing it bothers him, but I'm a ball buster too and this is just too good. "The sun is going down," I tell him as I pat his arm. "The sun is getting low. Shhh."

"You're dead," he jokes and then he lunges forward. His arms wrap around me and his fingers dig in my sides as he starts to tickle me.

My laughter is out of control but he doesn't let up. I squirm in his arms, remembering how he would do this to me when we were kids. I'm super freaking ticklish and I hated it then and I still do. "Truce. Truce!" I yell as Ben takes me to the floor.

His huge body lies on top of me and my hair is all over the place. I puff my breath, moving the strands that are covering my view.

"I haven't laughed like that in years," I confess.

"Years?"

"Yeah, I can't remember when, honestly. Maybe when Ashton did something stupid, but not like that."

He pushes his body weight up a little. "Didn't the dipshit you were going to marry make you laugh?"

"Harold? No. Not even a little."

His eyes harden a bit and then sadness fills them. "So you didn't laugh, didn't say you were happy, what else didn't you do?"

The question stuns me. He looks at me, his eyes probing for answers that I'm not willing to give him. The truth is, we didn't do anything. I was his dirty little secret. I lived under a cloud of lies and broken promises. He told me he loved me. He told me that all of it was necessary and I was so stupidly tied to that damn life list that I wouldn't relinquish.

Tears fill my vision, blurring Ben, who continues to stare down at me. "Gretchen?"

"Everything."

"Everything?"

"I did nothing. We didn't date or laugh. There were no nights of him picking me up. In fact, I've never even been on a date. I didn't have time for that in college and then Harold was the first guy I really dated." I say the last word in air quotes. "Which is a far stretch because it was meeting in secret, pretending we felt nothing, and sneaking around. I was the shadow in the dark that needed to stay hidden. He never met my family. He never did anything to be a part of my life until I demanded we either get married or end things. Then, we were engaged, he promised me light and then I was stood up on the most important date of my life. So when you ask what I didn't do...everything."

The sadness that was in his gaze is gone, now it's replaced with anger. "You don't deserve to ever be in the dark. You should've been the one thing in the world he couldn't wait to show off. He should've picked you up, planned a night you wouldn't forget, worried whether he should kiss you or not."

I hold my breath, waiting to wake up because no one has ever said anything like that to me. It's always been that this was how it was. I should be grateful that he was taking a risk on his career for me. God, I was so stupid.

But Ben looks at me like I'm...special.

His eyes move to my lips, keeping his gaze there. Is he going to kiss me? My belly fills with butterflies as I now feel what he described before. Then he lifts his hand to graze my cheek.

He's going to kiss me. He could right now and I don't know that I'd stop him.

"Ben." I say his name, unsure of what I want him to do.

The sound of my voice breaks the trance we were both under. He leans back with a quick shake of his head.

I feel the loss of his touch in my heart. I need a freaking therapist.

It was my wedding day a few days ago and now I'm thinking about and wanting another man to kiss me? I feel no sadness, no guilt. If anything, I feel like I want to crush my lips to his and have my way with him. There's something wrong with me.

He gets up. "I have an idea."

"You do?"

"Yup."

I wait for him to elaborate but he doesn't. "Are you going to share it?"

Ben smirks. "We're going on a date."

Okay. That's definitely not what I was expecting. "Excuse me?"

"A date. I'm going to pick you up tomorrow night and we're going to go out."

I laugh once, thinking he's kidding.

However, the look on his face tells me he's not. He's serious. And crazy.

No way am I going on a date.

With Ben.

Who I just wanted to kiss me.

"You're funny. We're not going on a date."

Ben puts his hand up. "Just listen. You haven't had a date or a real anything because you were with an asshat. So, when someone worthy comes around, you're going to be confused on what chivalry and all of what is supposed to go on during a real date. I think that it's important to know what to expect *and*," he says when I open my mouth to stop him, "if that guy doesn't do what I plan to do, you dump his piece of shit ass *immediately*. So I'll be over tomorrow at six."

I stand here unsure of what just happened. But I think I'm going on a date with Benjamin Pryce.

Chapter Seven

Ben

Why the fuck am I nervous? It's not a real date. It's me showing Gretchen what her douchefucker of an ex was too much of a pussy to do. Show her a good night where she's treated how she should've been all along.

Never been on date?

Ridiculous.

I need to man the fuck up and show her a date like she's never seen. I make my way to Catherine and Jackson's condo that they still own, where Gretchen is staying, and ring the doorbell.

It's been a long time since I've been here. I moved out about four months ago and I try not to think about the fact that she's sleeping in the same bed that I did.

Before I can focus too much on it, she opens the door wearing a pair of jeans and a shirt that hangs down on one side, giving me a view of her shoulder. Her blonde hair is swept to the side over the shoulder that isn't exposed.

She's beautiful.

Absolutely fucking breathtaking.

The last few years haven't been kind to me and I haven't been to myself either. When I lost my leg, I was fucking furious at the world. Sometimes I still am. But right now, I just want to fall to my knees and thank God for allowing me even just tonight to be with Gretchen.

"You look..." I stumble.

"Homeless?"

Definitely not the adjective I would've used. "What?"

She sighs. "I have all my stuff in storage until I find somewhere permanent. I wasn't really thinking of keeping out date clothes when I packed essentials. I mean, I think the jeans make my butt look good at least." She turns her perfect ass toward me and looks at it over her shoulder. "Right?"

I clear my throat, trying to wipe away the images of her bent over with my hands gripping it. "Very good."

Gretchen beams. "But this top sucks. Catherine had it in her closet and since she's in California, I borrowed it because well...she won't care."

I move closer. "You look beautiful, Gretch. Beautiful."

Her smile makes my heart beat faster. "Really? Are you sure? I haven't really heard...it's just..."

It's as if that's the first time anyone's ever told her how gorgeous she is. How the fuck did this guy ever let her go?

He's a fool, that's how.

"Thank you." Her hand rests on my forearm. "You look really good too."

"Let's head out," I say before I press her against the door and kiss her until she can't breathe.

We make our way to the car and she whistles. "Wow."

I'm a car guy. I love taking something old and making it look new. Liam and I work on our cars every weekend. My baby, Betty, is everything. Betty is a 1970 Dodge Challenger convertible. It's a metallic purple with a black roof.

Gretchen walks over, her fingertips graze the paint and I have to remember not to act like an idiot. This is a date. I have to not be ridiculous about my car.

"It's gorgeous."

"Betty, this is Gretchen."

"Oh, God!" Gretchen slaps her hand to her head. "You too? Jesus. I know Liam is a little insane about his car...Robert? Roberta?"

"Robin," I correct her.

"Right. So you're like that too? Seriously? You're how old and you're introducing me to your car?"

I shrug. "You're about to go inside her. I wanted you both acquainted."

Her jaw falls slack. "In case, what? In case she wants to kick me out?"

If she did, I would take Betty's side, but I don't say that. Since I would sound ridiculous.

"You never know."

Gretchen shakes her head like she can't believe this conversation.

"If it makes you feel any better, you're the first girl to ever ride in her."

"Really?"

"Really."

Gretchen steps close to me, her hip resting on Betty. "Why is that?"

Because you're the only girl I've ever given a fuck about.

Because you're the only girl I've ever thought about.

Because I fucking dreamed that one day this could be reality.

Instead of spouting shit and looking ridiculous, I tell her the truth. "Because no one else was worthy."

I pull the passenger door open, and she grins. "Good answer."

"Get in, babe. We've got a date to go on."

I close the door and walk around the back. This date is for her, not me. I tell myself that a few more times as I make my way to the driver's seat. I want to show her what it should be like because she never should've had to wonder.

"Ready?" I ask.

"Yes."

I'm glad one of us is.

* * * *

"You're taking me to a chick flick?"

"Of course I am."

"You're nuts!"

Did this guy never take her to a fucking movie? It was bad enough that through dinner she kept talking about how weird it was to be in public.

I've never wanted to kill someone as much as I want to with this guy. He not only made her doubt herself, but also gave her the lowest expectations possible. I want her to get everything she could ever want. She deserves that and more.

"No, I'm being a dude hoping at the end of the night you'd let me stick my tongue in your mouth. This is what happens on a date," I say with a hint of sarcasm laced in truth.

Gretchen laughs. "Most guys I know don't want to see this."

"You think I do?"

Hell no do I want to sit through two hours of some stupid movie where I'm going to want to punch not only the "hero" of the movie but myself by the end. However, this is what guys do for girls they want to woo.

And wooing is what is happening here.

"I feel bad for the guy who takes me out after tonight," she says and rests her head on my arm as we walk into the theater.

Yeah, me too because I'm going to kill him. No one else should ever get to know her like this, only me.

I stop moving when I think the last part. I'm not the right guy for her. I'm far from worthy. She's perfect, unmarred, not scarred or broken. Gretchen isn't walking around with a life's worth of anger because she's alive.

Nope. That's me.

"You okay?"

Shit. "Yeah, I'm good."

"We can see something else." Her voice is soft with a hint of sadness.

Damn it. Me and my fucking issues. "No. No way. I'm excited to see all this love and smiles."

Gretchen's smile is timid. "Seriously, Ben, we don't—"

"Stop it. This is a date. We're going to see a date movie and you're not going to try to fix this. You're going to just enjoy it, got it?"

I can see that it's eating her up inside. She wants to make everyone else happy but herself. I bet right now, if I said we were going to see some action movie, she'd do it just because it's what I wanted.

She's spent her entire life, and relationship to the douchefucker, worrying about everyone else's happiness instead of her own.

"Fine. You seem really firm on it, so we'll go see the sappy movie."

Good.

"Let's go. The previews are the best part and you need to

experience the awkward pre-date sitting."

She hooks her arm through mine and we make our way to our seats. One thing that the movie companies finally did right was reserved seating. It's nice not to have to try to get here thirty minutes early just to not be stuck in the front row.

We sit down and she grabs the popcorn. I forced her to share a drink with me, part of the fun is reaching for the cup at the same time, and the lights dim.

Now I just need to keep my hands to myself.

Chapter Eight

Gretchen

He's so close.

He's so close and all I want to do is reach my hand over and take his, but this isn't a real date. This is him trying to teach me, and I need to remember that.

It's not like he likes me. He feels bad.

I'm so stupid.

I can't believe I let myself start to wish otherwise. When I was getting ready today, I kept wondering if he'd think I was pretty or if he liked my hair up or down. I fussed over everything.

My nerves are shot and my muscles are tight. I'm crazy because this is Ben. The boy who used to eat dinner at my house every week because my mother likes him more than me. He's the kid who watched movies in my bedroom and made fun of me the entire time.

He makes a yawning noise, lifting his arms over his head and then around my shoulders.

I let out a giggle and lean close, my voice is a whisper. "Smooth."

His lips brush my ear. "Wooing. I'm wooing you."

I bite my lower lip to stop myself from laughing. "It's working."

"Good."

If this is how dates are supposed to be, I've been missing out. He's so sweet by opening doors, helping me out of the car, paying for the movie and snacks. I lift the arm rest between us, tucking my leg up and nestling into his chest.

His body locks and then releases a second later. I don't look up at him, instead I force myself to focus on the crappy movie playing. My pulse spikes when a few minutes later, his fingers begin to idly play with my hair. Almost as if he doesn't know it's happening.

This was our thing as kids.

We'd watch movies and snuggle.

Now we're adults. I'm ridiculously attracted to him, and this has danger written all over it.

The movie ends and I realize I missed the entire ending. I laid on his chest, with my eyes closed, enjoying the way his hands felt on me.

Pull it together, Gretchen.

"Did you like it?" Ben asks as we walk out.

"Sure."

He laughs. "I knew you weren't even watching!"

Shit. Now I'm busted. "It was stupid!"

"God you're still the same in so many ways. You never watched the movies when we were kids and you would pretend."

I definitely did that. I was comfortable then and apparently now.

"Whatever. You're the same too."

"How?"

I hook my arm in his as we walk. "You're still very sweet. You play with my hair. You still have no issue telling me what you think."

Ben snorts. "You still don't listen then and you're nuts if you think I'm sweet."

"Nope. You're wrong. You're very sweet."

"Doubtful."

"I know sweet Benjamin Pryce and you are a big teddy bear with a heart of gold. Now, how am I the same?"

"You still argue." Ben nudges me.

"Ha!" I laugh and then shrug. "That's an occupational hazard. I argue for a living."

Ben takes my hand in his. It's so innocent and sweet, and I pull it out.

"Sorry," he says with a hint of sadness.

What the hell is wrong with me? I'm so ridiculous. "No, I am. I'm sorry," I say, stopping in front of him.

"You don't have—"

"I do! Please, let me explain." I know this is going to go over like a ton of bricks but there's a reason I'm such a mess. "I told you how Harold and I had to spend our entire relationship in secrecy. Well, that was the same with touching. I could never hold his hand if we were walking like this. Just in case. Just in case someone from the firm or a client saw us. It was just reflex and I'm sorry."

Ben steps forward, his hand cups my cheek and my instinct is to move, but his other hand comes up, trapping me between his strong grasp. "You don't owe me an explanation, but I will say that I can't begin to understand how he could stop himself from touching you. I know you miss him and wish you were with him, but God, I don't understand it. I don't know how the man could keep any distance from you."

"There's something wrong with me," I confess. "That's the thing. It's clearly me."

Through this entire night there was something bothering me. Through dinner and then the movie I never once missed Harold. I wasn't wishing it was him instead of Ben. I didn't think about Harold other than to think how stupid he was.

"No, there's nothing wrong with you."

My hands wrap around his wrists, but he doesn't pull his hands down. "I just mean that I don't miss him. I was engaged to him, and I don't miss him. I haven't thought about him. I haven't wondered what he's doing or thought about how he must feel. Because I don't care. It's crazy. I mean, there has to be something wrong with me because no one doesn't miss someone they were going to marry a few weeks ago, right?"

Ben's eyes are filled with so much emotion. "There is nothing wrong with you, Gretchen. Nothing."

I shake my head and a tear falls. "I was going to marry a man I didn't love. I would've stood at that altar and said I do. All for what? To follow my plan? To fulfill some stupid idea I had about life? I would've done it. I would've spent the rest of my life with him, had those kids, lived that lie."

I look at him to give me the answer telling me I'm crazy. It would at least explain what's wrong with me. How could I not think about Harold? How is it that Ben is what consumes my thoughts at night?

There's something about him holding me that made me feel secure, which I haven't felt in a long time. Deep inside, I know that Ben will protect me, my heart, my feelings. Hell, he's doing it now. He isn't running and hiding for fear that someone might see us. No, he's taking me in his arms—in public.

His hands are out for me to hold, not making me a secret.

And then there's how my body reacts to him—which is a whole other problem. He's...Ben. He's the sweet guy who carried my books. The one who always made sure I didn't sit alone at lunch. He's always taken care of me, and he's doing it again.

Ben's voice is low and cautious, but underneath I hear something else that I can't name. "Thank God you didn't."

My heart races at the inflection in his voice. I want to ask him why he feels that way or said it at all, but instead, Ben wipes the tear from my cheek and takes a step back. "Now, no more talk about what's wrong with you. We have part two of the date. Okay?"

He puts his hand out, allowing me to take it this time. I nod, untrusting of my voice at this point, and put my palm in his. Knowing he might have just taken a part of my heart back again.

* * * *

The second part of the date is probably my favorite. Okay, it definitely is. Ben took me to the boardwalk. It's not like what I'm used to in New Jersey, but it reminds me a bit of home.

"You didn't have to do this," I say as we walk with his arm around my shoulder.

"Yes I did. You're a Jersey girl and I know all too well what we grew up doing."

"You left before all of that," I remind him.

"I still spent my summers at the shore, eating cheesesteaks at Midway and riding rollercoasters. And if I remember correctly, you and I spent time there too."

I smile as the younger version of us comes to mind. We were in eighth grade, right before he left, and my mom drove us down to Seaside Heights. There was something so simple about my generation when it came to living. We didn't have this insane fear that we would be taken or lost. We could go down that shore, walk the boardwalk as long as we were back before the lights were on or we checked in. I didn't have a cellphone and there were no tracking devices, but there was trust.

Ben and I were allowed to walk the boardwalk with our ten dollars, spending it on ice cream and the arcade.

"It was one of my favorite memories with you," I tell him.

"It was because of my impeccable kissing skills."

I laugh and playfully smack his stomach. "Please. You sucked. You were all tongue and braces."

Ben snorts. "You were no better."

"I was too."

"Nope. You were definitely one of my worst kissing partners."

I scoff and stop walking. "Is that so?"

"Sorry, babe, I just speak the truth."

"I'll have you know I'm a fantastic kisser."

"Doubtful. No one could improve that much," Ben tosses back with mirth in his tone.

I know for a fact I'm a good kisser. No one has ever complained before and the guys I was with always wanted more.

I'm taking that as a testament to my skill. I also know I'm walking into a trap, but the truth is, it's one I want to walk into.

I want to kiss him.

I want to feel his lips on mine as a grown woman.

There's not a doubt in my mind that he wants it as well.

"I'll prove it." I throw down the first gauntlet.

"No."

My stomach drops. Oh, God, I've been reading it all wrong. He really was just being nice and trying to show me a real date. He doesn't like me that way and I was so stupid just now. Damn it.

"Right," I say with wounded pride. I start to turn, but he grabs my arm, stopping me.

"No, you don't need to prove it." Ben takes one step, his hands returning to my face. He cups my cheeks, tilting my head to the side. "I'm going to kiss you. Right. Now."

And then he does.

But it's nothing like our first kiss. It's not fumbling, unsure, or soft. This kiss is powerful and full of passion. Benjamin Pryce kisses like he owns the world. My lips are molded to his and my hands grip his elbows. The heat from his touch is felt down in my toes.

I have never in my entire life been kissed like this.

When his fingers slide back into my hair I gasp, and he uses that opportunity to slide his tongue in. At the first feel of it against mine, I lose it.

He controls the tempo, moving swiftly and then slower, making me crazy in the middle of the boardwalk. People move around us, but I don't give a flying fuck. All I want is to drown in this man's warmth.

"You're so beautiful," he tells me and then his mouth is on mine again.

I move my fingers to his solid chest, feeling the muscles pulse underneath my touch.

God, he's so good at this.

I melt, my body molding to his in one of those movie type kisses.

He pulls back, giving me two chaste kisses and I stand here, eyes closed, savoring the best kiss of my life.

After another heartbeat, I open them, finding his deep brown ones looking down at me. Ben's lips turn to a sly grin. "So, do I still suck at kissing?"

"No. Definitely not."

He leans back down again, kissing me softly this time. "Neither do you."

Chapter Nine

Ben

My leg is killing me. I haven't pushed myself this hard in a long time. Not that I don't still go to the gym and keep up with my physical therapy, but I didn't think through my big plan for the day.

We walked the boardwalk, well, sidewalk. I don't know why Virginia Beach thinks pavement is a boardwalk. The entire name says it—board. But there are no boards. I wanted to take her down to the water, smell the ocean, hear the waves up close, but my fucking leg doesn't do sand.

She never asked once or made a comment. She didn't fuss over me either. It was nice. I felt—normal.

I roll over out of bed, massaging the muscles and putting lotion on the now red and inflamed skin.

"Fuck," I groan as it burns.

Today is going to suck.

I force myself to wake up and get ready. Once in the shower I close my eyes and Gretchen's face after our kiss is front and center.

She's so beautiful. The way she looked up at me like I just made her life worth living was humbling and almost brought me to my knees. After all this time it's as if the feelings I had for her just resurfaced like time never passed.

I think about the sounds she made and my cock hardens. My hands itch to touch her again, feel her silky skin beneath my rough fingertips.

Instead of touching her, I wrap my hand around my dick and start to jerk off.

Her face is all I see.

Her perfume is all I smell.

Her voice is all I hear as I continue stand to here, one hand on the wall, one on my cock.

I have no control as I think about her. I imagine it's her lips around me, the warmth of the water is her mouth and I come—hard.

I get out of the shower and my phone dings.

Gretchen: I had a really good time. Thank you.

Me: You're welcome. I did too.

Gretchen: I'll see you at the office?

How the hell I'm going to work beside her all day, I'll never know. I'm going to have to use every possible tactic I learned to keep my composure. Kissing her was a big mistake, but I can recover. I got her out of my system a few minutes ago. I should be totally fine. It'll be a walk in the park.

Me: I'll be there.

Gretchen: Good. I can't wait to see you. I keep thinking about our kiss and...I just thought you should know. It was really good too.

Yeah, work today is going to be a piece of cake.

* * * *

"I have a theory," Gretchen says as we sit at the table.

Me too, that I'm a complete idiot to think I wouldn't want another date with her. I thought I would show her a good time, go home, drink a beer and be done.

Instead I'm jerking off in the shower and thinking about how to get a second date with her. Not one to show her a good time, but because I want to show her that I want her.

I rub the back of my neck and focus on work. "What's that?"

"The contracts are all worded differently. I'm starting to think whoever was drawing them up was trying to give the client a loophole depending on what the company was doing. Look...” She points to a line in another contract. “...I’m fairly certain this line shouldn’t be here.”

I read it over, not really sure of what it means. “Why?”

“Because if we’re drawing up the contracts, which it appears we are, we wouldn’t want any possible openings for lawsuits. Thankfully, you guys are really good at what you do, so there hasn’t been a fuck up, but...”

“But you think someone was hoping for it?”

“Yeah, it’s the only thing that makes sense.” She gnaws at the end of her pen.

God, she’s gorgeous. Her blonde hair is down and curled at the ends today. She’s wearing a light pink top with a black skirt. I can’t stop looking at her legs, wishing they were wrapped around my waist.

It’s been almost two years since my divorce and I haven’t given a shit about women since Charity left. She fucked with my head so bad. I was only good enough for her when I was a SEAL. She loved the military life and wanted to bask in the glory that came with it. Not that I think there is much glory. It’s a lot of time away, fighting, dealing with being alone, but Charity enjoyed it. I’m just glad we never had kids.

I think about the words the bitch said when she signed the divorce papers, which left her with nothing.

“It’s fine, Ben. I don’t need your money because no one wants to sleep with only part of a man.”

“Ben?” Gretchen’s hand touches my arm. “Did you hear me?”

“No, sorry.” I shake my head, coming back to the present.

She gives a soft smile. “I asked if the lawyer who was drawing up the contracts is still on staff. I’d like to just poke around a bit.”

“He’s not, which is why Jackson needed you so quickly.”

Now I’m starting to wonder if there’s more. Why would the lawyer put any kind of loophole in? There should be nothing that would leave us open for a lawsuit.

“Okay,” Gretchen says, tapping her pen. “I just—”

“Have a weird feeling?”

She nods.

“Me too. Let’s go talk to Mark.”

We get up and I wince. My leg is screaming today. The skin is still raw from rubbing against my prosthetic more than usual.

“Are you okay?”

"I'm fine."

"You look like you're in pain..."

Then I hear Charity's words in my head again.

"I'm fine." My voice is sharper than I intended.

"Sorry."

Fuck. I didn't mean to snap at her. It's not her fault. "That was out of line. I'm fine, I'm just uncomfortable."

"Is it your leg?" Gretchen asks.

I don't want to admit defeat. In fact, I hate it. I've come to terms with my life for the most part, but I'm still pissed. I lost everything because of this injury. I'm tired of things being chipped away from me. There's no fucking glory in feeling weak.

"Let's just forget about this and deal with what we have to."

Gretchen looks like she's going to keep pushing, but she nods. "Okay, but," she says and presses her hand to my mouth, "if you insist on being stubborn, I understand because you always were an idiot, but if you're in pain, you should take care of yourself. I know all too well about neglecting yourself for the sake of appearances."

Her hand drops and her features are soft, just like my heart when it comes to her.

I was just a dick to her and she's worried about me. "Don't worry about me, babe. I've learned to endure through much worse pain."

Then Gretchen reaches up on her toes, her eyes on me asking a million questions. There's hesitancy, fear, excitement, and lust as her mouth inches closer. I don't move, allowing her the control over what she does. That's something she hasn't had in many years and if she wants this, she has to take the next step.

"I'm going to kiss you, Ben."

I stand like a statue. "I'm right here, babe."

Her hand rests on my chest as she moves slowly, measuring each breath and I have to lock my muscles to stop myself from hauling her to my body and crushing our lips together.

But I don't—I wait.

Dying a slow death.

Until our lips touch, and I remember what breathing feels like again—her.

Chapter Ten

Gretchen

"Thanks for doing this," Liam says as he lets me in the door.

"Not a problem. I love kids."

I enter their home and Natalie rushes down the stairs.

"Gretchen! You saved me, you have no idea!"

"Seriously, guys, it's babysitting, I'm happy to do it. Not like I have anything going on that I can't step away from."

My life...is boring. I sit around Jackson and Catherine's apartment, clean, sit some more, clean up again, and stop myself from texting Ben.

That's my life.

"Still, we appreciate it." Natalie smiles. "Liam promised me a date three weeks ago and then the kids got sick which led to the man-flu, which is a whole other type of disease."

I laugh. "Oh, I remember all too well when Harold got sick."

She rolls her eyes. "What is it with men? I get sick and I still function."

Liam clears his throat. "Umm, sweetheart, if you need to be reminded of that one time you were sick..."

"One time. One. Not the sniffles, I was on my death bed," she says with a challenge in her voice.

"See what I deal with?" Liam says to me.

"No way am I stepping in this one."

Natalie and Liam go over the basics of where everything is. Their home is color coded by child and in bins, which makes my crazy-organized-self happy.

There's a knock on the door. "Who the hell?" Lee looks at Liam and makes her way to the door.

When she opens it, my heartrate spikes.

There, in a pair of running shorts and a shirt with the arms cut off stands a very sweaty and very sexy Ben. I lean against the wall, needing the structure to keep me upright. The shirt clings to his chest, showing every muscle that I know is hiding under there. His shorts are baggy and for the first time, I get a glimpse of his prosthetic leg. All I can think is, damn. Damn him for being so hot. Damn my stupid hormones for kicking into high gear.

I bite my lip and rest my head to the side, hoping to keep myself from drooling.

"Hey, what's up?" Liam asks.

His eyes meet mine, watching me watch him. "Hey," he says to Liam but is looking at me. "I got your text about needing someone to watch the kids and was doing some exercises..."

"Oh, shit. I forgot I didn't send you a text saying Gretchen was able to help out."

It's been three days since we've seen each other. After the kiss we shared, he flew out to California to meet with Jackson. I didn't know he was back or what happened, but I've longed to see him.

Which is totally crazy.

Ben and I are a bad idea. I'm a little broken, he's a little angry—okay, a lot angry. I don't know anything about his past and while he knows some of mine, it's just stupid to get into anything.

And yet, I kissed him.

He's kissed me and all I want is to be in his arms again.

Natalie looks at Ben and then at me. "Ben, why don't you stay and help Gretchen?"

"Huh?" Liam asks.

"Yeah." She places her hand on his arm. "It would be great to know that there were two of you in case Shane wakes up. That way she's not alone. She's not really familiar with the area, and you know..."

"I'm sure she—" Liam starts but then stops when he catches her face. "...could use the help."

Ben's lips turn to a sly smile. "It's up to her."

Here's my chance to stop whatever this is. If I tell him to go, we can go back to being friends or colleagues and move on. It's what I should do. "Stay," I say, proving I'm a total idiot.

"Then I will."

There's a thickness in the air. Me asking him to stay and him agreeing to do so feels like some sort of admission or surrender, but yet a challenge at the same time.

Our eyes stay locked, neither of us willing to break the stare first.

"Great." Liam claps his hands together, causing us both to look away. "Shane is asleep and should stay that way, but you never know with him. Aarabelle is watching a movie, and will probably sucker you into doing something she shouldn't."

I nod. "Got it."

Liam turns to Ben. "Okay, and the most important thing though is don't use any kind of rope, tape, glue, or bungee cords to tie up a diaper. Trust me, it doesn't work."

Natalie rolls her eyes. "Not everyone is as extra as you, babe. I'm sure Ben can handle it."

"He's a single dude, we're not all that up to speed on babies. Plus, he's likely to break things, like the stupid tabs of a diaper."

"Thanks for the tip, Dreamboat."

"Anytime, Hulk."

The whole call sign thing to me is so fun. Sure, we call Ashton an idiot, but it's not really a call sign. I can only imagine what they'd come up with for the girls. I know Mark has given Natalie one, which is Sparkles and Catherine is Kitty, and apparently, I'm Jilted. Being a part of their team is supposed to have perks. I guess nicknames that make you want to scream is just one.

"Okay, any other questions before they start punching each other?" Natalie asks.

I shake my head. "I think we're good. I'll call or text if there is anything else."

Aarabelle comes out from the living room. "Gretchen! Yay! Uncle Ben!"

"Hey, Peanut!"

She runs to Ben. He scoops her up and she begins to squirm with a case of the giggles. "You're all sweaty!"

"I was exercising, which is something your Athair fails to do. It's why he's getting scrawny in his old age."

I love how Aarabelle calls Liam that. Since she's not his daughter, but he is her father in every way that matters, they wanted a name that meant something. Liam is very passionate about his Irish roots so they use the Gaelic term for father. It's sweet and special between them.

"Athair?" Aarabelle questions Liam. "Are you scrawny?"

His eyes narrow. "No. I'm stronger than your Uncle Ben, that's for sure."

"Uncle Ben has big muscles."

"And little brains."

Natalie steps in. "Aara, why don't you show Gretchen the movie you're watching?"

"Okay, come on Miss Gretchen, I'm watching *princesses!*"

I take her little hand in mine and smile. I really love this kid, she's so sweet and respectful. "I love princesses!"

"Me too!"

Natalie clutches her hands to her chest and mouths: thank you.

"Uncle Ben! You have to watch princesses too!" Aarabelle calls.

"I wouldn't miss it," he says with a laugh.

The front door closes and Ben makes his way in. Aara and I are sitting on the couch and he sits on the other side of her. She scoots closer to him and tosses her legs up onto mine. "I love Cinderella. She's the best."

Ben's gaze meets mine. "You know, Gretchen loved Belle when we were kids."

"Really?" she asks with her eyes wide.

"Yeah, I sure did. She was smart, independent, and had goals."

"She also loved a big beast."

"She did."

Aarabelle completely missed the entire reasons why I think Belle is a badass, but sure, love wins all and what not. At least to a six-year-old.

"Uncle Ben, you're big like the Beast."

Oh God.

He chuckles. "I think I'm bigger and scarier."

She shrugs and looks back at me and then leaps to her feet. "We can play princesses. You can be Belle, Uncle Ben can be the Beast and I'll be..." She seems to ponder what role she wants. "I'll be the pretty enchantress!"

"Aara..." Ben says and almost as if she knows that he's going to shoot down her dreams of being the enchantress, she juts her lip out.

Well played, kid. Well played.

"But." She tilts her head to the side. "Don't you want to play?"

"Fine," he grumbles. "You don't play fair."

She grins as if she's well aware of her power over these big, strong men. I could learn a thing or two from her.

Chapter Eleven

Ben

Aarabelle is finally asleep after an hour of Beauty and the Beast retelling by a six-year-old. I had to wear a blanket as a cape and hide in a closet where I was to stay until I could be nice. Then I wasn't allowed to eat because I said a curse word and needed to be punished. Of course, Gretchen, being the princess, was allowed to eat all the cookies she wanted as long as she shared with the enchantress.

After that, I was allowed out of the closet, but then she decided I needed to go for a walk outside to think about my temper.

She may be the cutest kid in the world but she has a warped sense of fairytales.

Gretchen sits on the couch, legs tucked underneath her with my cape around her.

"You cold?" I ask and she jumps.

"No, I'm okay now that I'm allowed back inside. You?"

"Well, being outside with no coat wasn't exactly fun, but at least I had my cape."

She laughs and snorts. "That was the best version of that fairytale I've ever seen."

"Which part did you like? The closet or making me watch you eat cookies?"

"Both were equally fun."

"Women."

Gretchen shrugs. "At least she knows how to manage you guys like a pro."

That she does. "Aara has had a bunch of men at her disposal to do her bidding since birth. None of us can deny her anything."

I'm fairly new to the crew, but that doesn't mean I love her any less. "She's very sweet."

"Yeah, she's the closest most of us will ever get to having a kid, so she sort of owns us."

"What do you mean?"

Having kids has never been on my list. Charity sure as hell didn't want them, which worked just fine for me. Not that I don't love kids, but I didn't want to have them deal with me being gone all the time. Then, when my marriage dissolved, I decided it was probably better. I can't exactly run around, lift and toss them in the air or be the kind of father I would've wanted.

"I just mean that kids aren't really in my cards. I'm happy just being a good uncle to the kids around me."

Gretchen's face falls slightly. "Oh, well...then it's a good thing you have Aara to spoil."

"Spoiled she definitely is, but she's a special kid. It's like she just knows what each of us need. The first time I met her, I had just gotten the job and she saw my leg. She ran over, hugged my good leg and asked if she could kiss my other leg since I had a boo-boo. After that I think she owned me."

Gretchen's hands cover her heart. "That's the sweetest thing."

It really was. That was the first time I thought maybe I wasn't unlovable. It was irrational to ever think it anyway, but when your wife leaves because your injury is so repulsive, you start to wonder.

Even now, there are times I question how any woman can look at me and not be repulsed.

Then I think about how Gretchen looks at me and I start to hope again.

"Well, there's at least one girl who loves me."

Her lips purse. "What happened with your wife?"

My hand grips the back of my neck and I try to squeeze the tension.

"You don't have to tell me, but..."

"No, there's not much to tell. I got injured and when I came back, she was different. It was like my injury destroyed the vision she had.

Charity was vain, selfish, and wanted the glory that she got by saying she was a SEAL wife. I didn't see it before we were married or maybe I didn't want to. Our divorce was ugly, like her personality, and I haven't heard from her since."

"She left you because you were injured?" There's no mistaking the disgust in her voice. "Seriously? Were you mean when you got back? Or maybe something else because that is—horrible."

I wish I was mean. Before I was sent back to the States, I actually had a very long talk with the Chaplain. He explained that a lot of marriages and relationships suffer after injury and why. We spoke about how to channel the anger into the rehab and not at the people who loved and cared for me. Charity never saw my despair. I hid it, kept it buried, and did exactly what he said when it came to exerting my energy in the right places. Turned out it didn't matter because my wife didn't care regardless.

"Some people show their true colors after the ink is dried," I say with a sneer.

"I think your ex and Harold could be long-lost cousins."

I laugh once. "Probably. Maybe we could set them up."

"Can I ask you something else?"

"Anything."

For some reason, talking about this with Gretchen doesn't hurt as much as it usually does. I want to be open with her, tell her the truth, and I crave the same with her. I want her to trust and bare her soul to me. Which is fucking ridiculous because we're not the same people as we were almost twenty years ago. Things have changed, appendages lost, time slipped away and I'd be a fool to think there's a chance here.

"Do you think I'm an idiot?"

Her question stuns me. "What?"

Gretchen tucks a blonde strand behind her ear. "For living the way I did, agreeing to marry a man who kept me hidden. When I say all of it out loud, I feel like such a dumbass. I'm not a stupid person, but when it came to him, I was."

I hate that she thinks she has the blame on this. He was the fucking idiot, not her.

"You're no more of an idiot than I am for trusting my ex-wife. We're the ones better off without them. If they didn't leave us then we wouldn't be sitting here right now."

Her voice is soft and wistful. "And that would be sad for both of us. I'm much happier...right now, with you, than not..."

We both move closer, almost like magnets that can't stop ourselves. With each breath, our bodies pull nearer.

"I missed you when I was gone, which is crazy, right?"

She shakes her head. "No. I missed you too."

My gaze drops to her lips and I can feel her breath as we both breathe harder. "I think about you all the time," I confess.

Gretchen's hand reaches out, touching my cheek. "Ben?"

"Yes?"

Her chest rises and falls, the questions swirling in her eyes. "Shut up and kiss me."

"Yes, ma'am."

And then my lips are on hers and my heart in her hands.

Chapter Twelve

Gretchen

My phone rings and Ashton's face pops on.

"Hey," I say as I grab my bag, rushing out of the house.

Ben and I have a date. One that I planned and I need to get supplies. Instead of going out, I'm going to cook for him and hopefully much more than that.

"Hello to you too, remember me? Your best friend in Jersey?"

"How could I ever forget?"

"Well, according to Liam and Quinn, you've been rather busy with a very handsome man."

Damn it. My cheeks burn even though no one can see. Last night was incredible. A lot of walls were brought down, but having Natalie and Liam walk in to Ben and me making out on their couch wasn't the highlight of my life.

They thought it was hilarious, but I was mortified.

"Can no one keep secrets?"

She laughs. "Not in that group."

"Quinn, huh?"

"Don't try to change the subject."

Ashton is relentless when there's information she wants. "Okay, here's the Cliffnotes. Ben and I went on a fake date which turned into more of a real date than I think either of us expected. Then I kissed him because I can't seem to stop myself and after that we were babysitting and I asked him to kiss me. There you go."

"So you like him?" she asks with a softness to her voice.

"I do. Which is a little crazy, right?"

"Why? You were with a guy who was unworthy for so long, Gretch. You deserve to have some fun and if Ben is just that, then okay. If it's more, even better."

"But," I sigh, knowing this is a bad thing to admit. "What about my list? Ben doesn't really fit in since he doesn't want kids. He has no intention of ever getting married again thanks to his shrew of an ex-wife. I don't want to make the same mistakes I made with Harold by trying to fit him into something he doesn't want to do."

I think that's where my fault lies. I wanted to get married, have kids, and follow what I thought was a brilliant plan. By doing that, I was so hellbent on that timeline that I didn't see Harold wasn't the right guy to plug in. He told me, showed me a million times but I couldn't accept it.

His epiphany might have hurt in the worst way, but had I paid more attention, I would've seen it coming a mile away.

"Oh, Jesus Christ!"

"No, listen, I know you think it's stupid and my lists are dumb, but they keep me grounded."

I can picture Ashton banging her head on something. "Gretchen, for the love of God, lists are great for grocery shopping, but not life! Who fucking cares if he never wants to get married or have kids? Nothing is saying you have to have a relationship, just have some damn fun."

"That's the thing. I need my list because the truth is, I don't care about any of that when I'm with him. I don't know that I can just have fun with him! I don't know if I can walk away..."

Ashton falls silent. After a few seconds her voice is calming and almost sad. "You like him."

And that's the problem. I like men who don't want the same things as me and in the end I'll be the one disappointed. "More than I should."

"Then just feel it. Allow yourself whatever comes because in my expert opinion, that doesn't happen often and to those few that have felt it...they're all exactly where they should be."

I think of Catherine and Jackson, Natalie and Liam, Mark and Charlie. All of them found someone they didn't expect or hope to find and they're blissfully happy.

"And if he ends up hurting me?"

"You'll survive it. You're strong, beautiful, resilient, and you're smart as hell. Any man who walks away from you is a fucking idiot."

I laugh. "You're not so bad yourself."

Ashton snorts. "Please, I'm a fucking headcase. I can't figure out what I want, who I should be with, all I know is that I want a family. I want to have babies and love but I can't seem to find anyone who wants to share that life with me."

I feel bad for her. She's been in love with Quinn Miller for the last two years. Whether she wants to admit it or not. His life just isn't built for long distance and she won't give her career up. It's the one thing she has control over and Ashton needs that. They're at a stalemate and until one of them is willing to bend, they're just breaking.

"Quinn loves you, Ash," I defend him. Quinn definitely wasn't my favorite person in the beginning, but I think it was just the definition of their relationship that I struggled with. They had some weird agreement where they could live how they wanted when they were apart, but nothing serious. I'm not a traditionalist, I mean, I was fucking my boss in secret for years, but still. It was just too...weird.

The more time I was around Quinn and Ashton as a couple, the more I got it. It was the only way they could reconcile their feelings. By allowing each other freedom, they were able to find a way to make it work, until recently.

"I know he does. Even if he doesn't know he does. It doesn't matter, though. None of it does if we can't find a way to be together. He has the military and I have my job. He's deploying in a week anyway, so there's no finding a way."

I hear the pain in her voice and decide to let it drop. "I get it."

"Anyway, we're talking about you and Ben."

"No, we're done talking about that."

"Answer me this." She pauses. "If Ben fit on your list, would you date him?"

"Without question."

"Then write a new list."

* * * *

Ben is on his way. He should be here in about ten minutes and I'm staring at my notepad. On top is my header: Gretchen's Life List.

Under that...it's blank.

For the first time in my adult life, I don't know what to write.

I don't have a plan or an idea on where to go. There are no rules right now. I can do anything, live anywhere and choose something other than what I always thought.

Some might feel very liberated. I feel like I can't breathe. The lack of order isn't welcome.

A year ago, my list was solid and workable. Now, there's too much uncertainty. Is marriage even what I want? Then there's the fact that all I keep thinking about is Ben. Each time I go to write, he is the first thing I want to put down, which is fucking insane.

Harold never made my list. He was just who was going to fill in that slot.

A knock at the door causes me to jump.

"Shit," I mutter, pushing the book under some papers so he doesn't see it, and I try to collect myself as I walk to the door.

I close my eyes, hand on the door handle, release a deep breath, and smile. "Hey," I say as I open it.

"Hello, gorgeous." Ben's deep voice washes over me. "These are for you."

In his hand is a beautiful bouquet of daisies.

Daisies. "How did you...?"

"Are they not your favorite anymore?"

"They are, but I can't believe you remembered."

Ben looks at me like I'm a wounded animal. "Why wouldn't I?"

Because it's been so long. Because my stupid fiancé didn't even know daisies were my favorite. Each year, I'd get lilies or roses as he'd tell me he knew how much I loved them—which I didn't. I hate lilies. They're too strong in fragrance and give me headaches. Roses are pretty, but that's what you put on a casket. Morbid, I know, but after my Nana passed away, roses became associated with death.

Daisies, though, they're bright and airy. They're what little girls pick petals from and dream of love. They make me smile.

"It's just...very sweet. Thank you, Ben." I lean up on my very tippy toes and press a kiss to his cheek. "Come in, I made food."

He looks as though he wants to say more, but he nods and enters the house.

Jackson and Catherine's place is cute and quaint. It's a little beach bungalow a few blocks off the beach. They bought it a year ago when Catherine was visiting on one of their walks to the lighthouse. She said it was fate and needed it. Jackson, not being able to ever resist his wife, bought it immediately and spent two weeks fixing it up.

While the size isn't anything great, it has the most spectacular view of the lighthouse where she fell in love with Jackson Cole.

"I haven't been here since I got my place," Ben says as he looks around.

"What do you mean?"

Ben's smile makes my stomach clench. "I lived here before I found my place. Jackson and Cat sort of use this for the Virginia Beach crew as temporary lodging when we're not sure we're staying."

"But you did."

He takes a step closer and nods. "I did. Are you planning to?"

My initial though is, *yes*. Yes. I want to stay. I feel more alive since being here than I have in my whole life. More than that, I want him. I want to know why he was the first thing I kept thinking of when I was going to make my list.

"Do you want me to?"

"Yes."

There was no hesitation. Instead of asking him the questions that I want to know, I smile and shrug. "Well, I guess we'll see then."

"I guess so. It smells good," Ben says as he lifts his head toward the kitchen.

"Oh shit!" I yell, remembering I have sauce on the stove.

I rush in, praying the bottom didn't burn. I've made my Nana's sauce a million times and the key is going slow, not rushing, and adding everything in stages. It's a process. One that I've been at since nine this morning. Nana used to tell us that a good sauce was only good if there was love and time put into it, like life.

I used to think she was nuts and beg her to get a jar down to save us all the headache, but she would slap me with the wooden spoon at the mere mention of it. To her, sauce was how she showed her love.

I scrape the bottom, lift the spoon, and almost weep when there's nothing black or stuck. It would've destroyed the entire day's worth of work.

"Everything okay?"

I smile at him and nod. "Thankfully everything is okay. I'm glad I had the burner on so low."

"Did you make me Jersey food?"

"I did."

Ben takes a step closer and wraps me in his big arms. "You're the best."

I look up, my arms trapped at my sides. "Well, I figured you've been without for a while."

His arms drop and he kisses my nose as if it's the most natural thing to do. "I have. Your family always made Sunday my favorite day."

"They still do that, you know?"

I make my way back over to the pot, dipping in the spoon and tasting it. Perfect.

I turn the burner off and drain the pasta. Once the meal is plated I carry it over to the little table that fits in the corner.

He sits in the chair and shakes his head. "Your family amazes me. Mine was nothing like them."

"Crazy?"

"Loyal."

We had very different upbringings. His family barely spoke and really only saw each other on the holidays. Mine is obtrusive and constantly demanding time. Since I've moved down here, my mother has been up my cousin's ass, but leaving me alone. She's still pissed at me for leaving and also not repenting for my sins.

She drives me nuts.

"Well, they're also hot-headed and quick to give you the silent treatment."

"Not how I remember them," he says with a hint of awe. "They were always the best."

"They are...when they don't suck and want to tell you how to live."

He shoves a bite in his mouth and moans.

"Good?"

Ben nods. "Incredible."

I beam at the compliment.

We eat, chatting a little about our families, and he laughs hysterically when I recount my mother's horror at my being a heathen.

"It's not funny!" I slap his arm playfully.

"It kind of is."

"She was horrified."

"I'm more surprised she really believed you were a virgin." Ben stands, grabbing the plates, and walks over to the sink.

"Well, in her defense, she'd never known anything about Harold and I. So it's not like she ever saw me with men. I'm sure she thought I wasn't dating so I couldn't have sex then. I already told you I didn't really have dates, flowers, or anything to indicate there was someone special in my life. Then I was engaged and left because clearly I wasn't worth marrying."

Ben places the plates down a little too hard and the sound causes me to jump.

"Are you okay?" I ask.

He walks away from the sink and heads right to me. "No."

"No? What did I say?"

His eyes are filled with anger and I don't know what I did to upset him. "You said you weren't worth marrying."

"Well, it's true."

He moves closer and I take a step back. "The fuck it is!"

I don't know why he's so upset about this. It's the truth. I wasn't worth it to Harold. I wasn't even worth a real explanation or the respect of doing it until twenty minutes after I should've already been saying my vows.

When I start to back away more he grips my arm, pulling me against him, and tilts my head up using his thumb.

Our eyes stay on each other's as heartbeats pass between us. "You should've been given flowers all the time. He should've been running to the church to marry you. Not a single minute with you should've been taken for granted. There is nothing unworthy about you, babe. Not a single fucking thing. You should've been worshiped, adored, and revered."

My heart pounds so hard in my chest. "And would you have done that?"

His mouth slowly moves toward me. "I would do everything for you."

Chapter Thirteen

Gretchen

I hear the words, see his mouth move, but I don't know how to take them in.

"What are you saying?"

Ben starts to lower his mouth to mine. "I'm saying that I want you. I want to love you. I want you to give us a chance and I want you to let me."

"For how long?" I ask the question because I need to steel myself. "If it's only for tonight, just tell me."

He shakes his head, his nose grazing mine. "Not just tonight, Gretchen. But I won't make you promises until I know *I'm* worthy of you. I will never lie to you or make you question how I feel."

"Why do you think you're unworthy?" My voice is soft and barely audible.

"Because you're not the only one who is broken."

My heart beats against my ribs, loud and full of so many things. I don't know what this means, but I know that Ben will catch me if I fall. He won't lie or treat me with disregard. He's strong enough to accept me for who I am.

I reach my hand up, grazing the scruff on his face. "You're not broken."

His hand grips my wrist, bringing it to his lips, pressing a kiss right where my pulse is. "That's where you're wrong, but you might just be healing me."

I lift up on my toes, bringing our lips together in the softest kiss, but still filled with so much emotion I could cry. His hands wrap around my waist and then I'm flush against him.

My mouth opens and our sweet kiss is gone. Now it's passionate as both of us push the other for power. His tongue duels with mine.

It's everything.

It's a battle of wins and losses but I don't care which side I'm on because neither is really a loser. He kisses me as though he can't possibly get enough, and I match him in unbridled desire.

I break away and we both pant. "I didn't mean to push you."

My eyes meet his and I hope he sees the truth. "You didn't. I just want more. I want you, all of you. I always have."

"Gretchen." My name falls from his lips as both a prayer and a curse.

"Please. I want you to make love to me, Ben." I kiss him before he can deny me. "I want you to show me what I've been missing. Show me."

I stand here, more exposed than I've ever been. My clothes may be on, but my soul is exposed for him. I want him.

"Fuck," he groans and then our mouths are on each other.

Our hands explore each other, mine grazing over his massive chest, feeling each of the planes and ridges. We start to move and then my back hits the wall. He uses his size to dominate me, and I love every second.

Kissing him has become my new favorite thing.

My fingers dig into his shoulders as he dives his tongue into my mouth. I swear, if he fucks anything like he kisses...I'll be ruined.

I need to feel his skin. I want to touch him, make him feel as out of control as I do. I move to the hem of his shirt and push it up.

"Gretchen," he moans as I try to lift the shirt, but he anchors me against the wall, giving me no room to move.

I try again, but he grips my wrists.

"I can't," Ben says and takes three steps back.

Shame and mortification wash over me. He doesn't want me. I begged him and he didn't want to go there with me.

"I'm...yeah, no, I get it. You never said...I'm stupid." Each word stings with such sadness. I thought he wanted this as much as I did, but again, I read everything wrong.

Just like before.

"Stop." Ben's voice is thick with emotion.

A tear falls down my cheek and I hate myself for being vulnerable.

"Don't cry." He moves so quickly I couldn't even react. Ben's hands cup my face as another stupid tear slides from my eye. "Please, I do want you. I want you more than you can even imagine."

I shake my head, trying to dispel the words. "You don't have to say it."

"No. I do." I'm not sure who he's trying to convince, but it sounds more like himself. "I have to tell you. I've loved you for as long as I can remember. I've thought about making love to you in every fucking position possible. And now...you're in my arms, telling me you want the same thing, and..." Ben runs his hands down his face, moving away from me. "...and I'm part of a man."

What? I don't even understand what that means. "Part of a man?"

"Yes! Fuck, Gretchen! I'm missing a part of me!" he shouts, pointing down to his leg.

"You think that makes you less of a man?"

"Of course it does! She even fucking told me it did."

My God, what did that bitch of a woman do to him? How dare she make him think his injury made him less of anything? He's the kindest person and has endured so much pain. Ben isn't less, he's more.

I take a step closer, keeping my eyes on his. "You are not less, Benjamin Pryce. You are more of a man than anyone I've ever been with. More kind, more loyal, more loving." I move slowly, measuring each step, needing him to hear me. "You have given me more joy in the last few weeks than I've felt in years. Each time you kiss me, I think about how many years I've wasted on anyone but you. As impossible as it seems, you've broken down the hurt girl that's lived inside of me, showing me how much *more* there should be."

Ben goes still, his eyes watching me, and I pray his heart is hearing the words because they're the absolute truth. There are so many emotions in his gaze that it stuns me. However, the most prevalent is fear.

"When I look at you," I continue softly, "I don't see anything missing other than time we could've had. I want you more than anything. I want you to touch me and I damn sure want to touch you.

Do you want me? Do you want...us?"

His emotions are unreadable, but then his hand reaches out, tucking the hair behind my ear. "More than anything."

"Then take me. I'm here," I say, pulling my own shirt off, baring myself to him. "I'm yours." My bra falls to the floor.

"You're perfect."

And that's where he's wrong. "Perfection is an illusion that we cast to make ourselves think we're less than someone else. I'm not perfect, but I'm who I am. I have flaws." I reach for his shirt again, moving more slowly this time, I hold the bottom. "I'm scarred. But when you look at me, do you see them?"

"No."

I lift the shirt, pulling it up, and he lets me.

"No, because that's what love is."

Love allows each person's flaws to fade into the background, giving us only the beautiful parts.

My fingers trace against the skin, hating that he worried I wouldn't want him or see him as something less than.

"And what do you see, Gretchen?" Ben asks as I move my hands toward his neck.

I look into his eyes, allowing him access to everything I'm feeling. "I see a hero, my hero."

Ben doesn't hesitate. He grabs my face, bringing our mouths together. I kiss him, hoping to take the pain away, but still refusing to remove my hand from his chest.

I feel the muscles tense beneath my touch, but then they release after a moment. Almost as though he finds trust with each movement.

I slide both hands up farther, feeling more of the damage from the explosive, but it's just part of the story of who he is. He's the man that fought through whatever horrors he saw to come back here. The man who endured pain from the betrayal of the one person who should've loved him through it.

Instead of becoming mean and angry that the life he had was lost, he's been gentle and sweet. Ben didn't have to take me on a date, watch movies, text me, or make me smile. There was no take in this relationship, all he did was give. I thank God his ex-wife let him go because if she had seen the man he is, truly seen him, I wouldn't have him here with me.

His lips move to my neck, kissing their way down to my shoulder. "You have no idea how much I want you."

I'm pretty sure I do.

My head falls back, allowing him more access. "You have no idea how badly I do."

His eyes find mine and the desire that shines through is heart stopping. "Come," he says, taking my hand and leading me toward the bedroom.

"I'll follow you anywhere."

I mean that with everything inside of me.

Chapter Fourteen

Ben

Her hand is in mine and my heart is in hers.

I haven't been a monk since Charity, but none of those girls mattered. I didn't give a shit if my scars offended them or my leg disgusted them. This time, it's different.

Scary.

We enter her room and she turns, her arms around my neck, and kisses me, erasing the thoughts I was having. Right now, all I can think about is how amazing she feels, how soft she feels against me, and how much I want her.

My fingers grip her hips and then I slide my hands up to her breasts. They're the perfect size. Not too big and not too small. The wolf in me grins. "Does this feel good?" I ask as I roll her nipple between my finger and thumb.

"Yes."

"Do you want more?"

Her eyes meet mine. "I want it all."

"Good answer."

My head dips down and I lick around her nipple before taking it my mouth, sucking before I move to the other. She doesn't have to tell me if she likes it. The long moans and the way her fingers are gripping my hair tell me all I need.

I lift my head, knowing for the rest of what I want to do she needs to be in the bed. I move us that way, touching all the skin that is exposed to me.

I'm not sure what I did in my life to deserve her, but I'm so grateful.

I loved her once, lost her, and now I have her back and there's no way I'm letting go.

Gretchen climbs up backwards on the bed and I stare down at her. "Scoot all the way to the end."

"Why?" she asks, her blue eyes full of questions.

"Because I want to taste you and I need the room."

Her cheeks turn red, but she does as I ask. I remove her pants, and my heart begins to race when I look at her laid out before me. "You are fucking magnificent." I don't give her a chance to rebuke me, I lean down and swipe my tongue against her center.

I use my tongue to draw circles against her clit, listening for cues as to what she likes. I use different pressure, licking, sucking, and then she begins to grind against my face, setting a pace she prefers. Wanting to make her lose it, I finger her, mimicking how I wish it was my dick inside of her.

"Ben!" She yells my name and I continue to drive her crazy. "Harder!"

I could explode right here. Having her be aggressive and go after what she wants turns me on even more.

Far be it from me to deny her what she wants. I pump harder and suck at the same time, and then the most glorious thing happens— Gretchen explodes.

I watch as I keep flicking her. Her back is bowed, hands fisting the comforter, and she moans my name over and over.

She leans up onto her elbows, her eyes soft, her voice even. "You have to tell me...just tell me what you need."

"Just don't look away," I tell her as I get to my feet.

"Never," Gretchen vows.

I remove my pants, waiting for the moment she breaks her promise. As they fall to the floor, Gretchen's gaze is unwavering. She stays looking at me, then I drop my boxers, and her jaw goes slack.

"Holy shit," she mutters and I know it's not my leg she's talking about.

"That didn't get injured," I say with a brow raised.

"Thank God for that."

"I need to take it off."

She nods.

I turn, sitting on the bed, using this small break to collect myself. I remove my prosthetic and then I feel her lips on my back.

"If you're going to look away," she say between kisses, "then it's only fair I can touch while I wait."

Her hand glides down my chest and her other one goes down to my cock. Her tiny hand grips me and starts to pump.

"Fuck," I groan as she continues to jerk me off.

"I want to taste. Now. Lie down for me, babe."

I shift onto the bed, using my arms and good leg to get me there. Gretchen doesn't take her eyes from mine as she slides down my body and then wraps her lips around my cock.

I don't even think about the fact that my leg is exposed. There's no time to worry. Not a second to spare at the unease that I have when a woman sees it for the first time because all coherent thought goes out of my mind as she takes me deep.

"Jesus!"

She moans around my dick, making me even harder than I was before. Each time she comes up, she uses her tongue to rim me. It's fucking heaven and hell at the same time.

Then she cups my balls, rolling them around, and I have to start focusing or I'm going to embarrass myself.

"Gretchen, baby, you have to stop or..." I give her the sign by tapping her head. "Baby."

She goes down once more and then comes up. She kneels to the side of me, and I grip her hips, pulling her on top. Without a heartbeat, Gretchen swings her leg over, straddling me, and then sinks down.

"Oh my God." Her head falls back, hair falling down her back, just brushing my hands.

Every time I think she can't get any more perfect, she does. Right now, she's a goddess.

And then she begins to ride me, taking me to heaven.

Chapter Fifteen

Gretchen

Making love to Ben was a million times different than anything I've ever felt before. After, we fell asleep in each other's arms. However, now, I have an empty bed and I'm not sure if he left.

I get up, toss a T-shirt on and head toward the kitchen.

"Shit!" I hear his deep voice and pause.

There's some banging, more curse words, and then something that sounds like eggs cracking.

Oh, Lord.

"Good morning," I say as I peek my head around the wall. "You doing okay?"

He chuckles and shakes his head. "I really suck at cooking. I was attempting to be cute and again, woo."

"You wooed enough, babe."

Ben steps over and wraps his arms around my middle. "Yeah?"

"I think so."

"Good. Maybe we can woo again tonight?"

How different is this man from the last? It's like night and day. I would've been rushed out, just in case someone might have seen us or called. If the phone rang, he would rush out. For a while, I wondered if he was married, but...well, I can investigate like every other woman when she's on a mission.

"I'd really like that, Ben."

He smiles down at me. "I really like you, Gretchen."

"It's a good thing that you're so good at the wooing, then."

"Damn right it is."

I lift up at the same time he leans down and kisses me.

"I could get used to this," I say against his lips.

"I really hope you do." His phone rings, breaking the moment. Whatever the ringtone is causes Ben to flinch. "I have to take this."

"Okay, I'll clean up."

Ben moves to his jacket, pulling his phone out and I can see the stress in his back. He's tense and keeps clenching his hand.

"Pryce." His voice is clipped. He starts to pace, and I quickly move things around the kitchen. "Yes. I understand. Does Mark know?" He nods. "Okay. How long ago did we hear from them?" A long pause. "Has anyone had any contact since then?" He closes his eyes, and I move toward him.

Something is wrong.

Ben shakes his head. "I'll be on a plane in twenty minutes. Don't touch anything until I get there."

He doesn't say anything to me as he makes his way to the bedroom. "Ben?"

"I have to go."

"I understand that, but is there anything I can do? Are you okay?"

His eyes are filled with regret. "I don't know. My team is missing. They didn't check in last night and I didn't fucking know because I didn't hear the phone ringing a hundred times!"

"I'm sorry."

Guilt fills me because he didn't answer because we were too busy with each other. I don't know anything about the military, other than what I've dealt with Cat and Ashton, but I know loyalty. I understand the bonds of friendship and how hard it is when someone you care about is hurting.

I would do anything for Catherine and Ashton and I imagine it's a lot like that.

"I'll call when I can."

"Okay."

Ben tosses his shirt over his head and heads to the door. He doesn't leave, though. He turns, grabs me in his arms and kisses me. "Last night meant everything to me. I'm not leaving because I want to."

I touch his chest. "It was everything for me too. Go. Go be badass and take care of your friends."

He kisses me once more and then he's gone.

* * * *

"Tell me everything!" Catherine squeals and grabs my hand.

As happy as I am that my best friend is here, I was not prepared for an interrogation.

"Uhh..." I'm at a loss for words. *Somehow*, she and Natalie figured out that Ben didn't answer his phone because he was with me. "Nothing really to tell."

"The hell there's not!" Catherine scoffs. "His car was outside the house all night. He left from there. *Sooo...*"

"So, none of your business."

She and Natalie share a look and then she starts in. "Do you know how many Froghoppers have tried to get Ben since he's been back? The line is long, my friend."

I'm not sure if that's supposed to make me feel better or worse. "Okay..."

"I'm just saying landing a SEAL is always their goal, but an injured SEAL is gold to those bitches."

"There are women who troll SEALs?" I've never heard of such a thing. Why? What's the end game?

Natalie snorts. "Girl, they don't care if they're married or not. If they have the trident, they're in. You know about my ex-husband..."

She's so much better off. Liam loves Natalie beyond reason. Her first marriage was hard, but what she went through in the last few years has been impossible. However, she found a man who not only adores her, but her daughter.

"You definitely got the better end of that bargain," I joke.

"For sure, but I'm just saying that it's part of the shit women do. Hell." Natalie claps her hands. "His ex-wife is a Froghopper! She left him as soon as he wasn't titled the way she wanted. She's...not liked."

I'm glad she isn't somehow embedded in this group. Although I know these women and they would never be okay with the way she treated Ben.

"Did you know her?"

"Unfortunately. Ben and Liam were on the same team. I don't know if you know that."

I shake my head.

"That's how he ended up at Cole. When he was injured, they offered him an admin job, allowing him to stay active, but, for these guys, that's the equivalent of death. I know it's dramatic, believe me." She rolls her eyes. "I tell Liam all the time how ridiculous they sound, but they're men who want to serve. They need to be out there, doing the things no one else can or most of the time want to. Having to sit at a desk and watch his brothers go out to do combat would eat him alive. Which is why I don't think Jackson understands what he gives to guys like Ben."

Catherine smiles and her eyes fill with love. "He really loves them. It's why we were on a plane in the middle of the night to get here."

"They're devoted to the company, too, Cat."

"I saw it today." I jump in, wanting her to know how Ben felt. "He was distraught about not being there for the guys."

"That's how they are. They're loyal to a fault to their team. I just wish they were all to their wives, but that's another day," Natalie says with a hint of frustration. Then she takes a sip of her coffee, tucking her legs under her. "But let's get back to you and Ben bumping uglies."

The three of us sit on Lee's deck, drinking coffee, laughing, and talking about the men in our lives. There's no point in trying to keep it from them, they'll just pester me or worse, ask Ben. After a few hours of chatting, her kids demand her attention, so Cat and I head out.

"You know," Catherine says with hesitation, "in the last few years, I felt like you've disappeared. I understood that you loved someone and there are times where love can consume you, taking you away, but with you, I didn't see that. It wasn't like you were deliriously happy. You were...distant. Today was the first time I felt like my best friend was herself again."

"Cat..."

"No, I'm just saying, maybe you getting stood up at the alter was the best thing for you."

I let out a small laugh and shake my head.

The thing is, I agree with her. If I had married Harold, I would be a shell of who I feel like I am right now. I'm free. I'm alive. I'm happy and that has to do with a choice that wasn't mine being made for me.

"Maybe his epiphany was actually good."

"I think it was."

"I have to thank you and Jackson, though. If it weren't for this job, I would've stayed in New York, worked for some other law firm, hating life, and probably pining over a man who didn't love me."

Catherine takes my hand. "I'm so happy for you, Gretch. I'm so glad you found Ben, too. It's like a love story we dream of."

She's such a romantic at heart. I love her for it.

"It was like time never passed for us, you know?"

Her phone rings and she looks down. "It's Jackson, give me one second."

I nod.

Catherine talks for a few moments and then she goes silent for a few heartbeats, before her eyes meet mine and I can see the fear. "I understand. I'm with Gretchen now." Jackson must speak and her hand covers her mouth. "We'll be there as soon as we can."

"Cat?"

She hangs up, tears fill her vision and I know. Deep in my gut, I know it's Ben.

"We have to go."

"Where?"

She straightens her back. "It'll be okay. We just have to go."

I grab her arm. "Tell me."

"It's fine."

"Then tell me!"

Her hands grip my wrists. "There was an incident. Ben was hurt, but Jackson doesn't have information. We need to go. Okay?"

My heart seizes and I want to fall to the ground. He can't be hurt. He's not even in the military. Ben shouldn't have been out there anyway. Just a few hours ago we were fine, happy, making love.

"Is it bad?"

Her lips purse. "I don't know. I know it's enough Jackson wanted us to get on a plane."

I get in the passenger seat, close my eyes, and say a prayer to let him be okay. I would never recover from losing him.

Chapter Sixteen

Ben

"Well no one told you to be a fucking hero!" Mark grumbles as I wince, trying to move in the damn hospital bed.

"Fuck you."

"No thanks, I'm all booked up with fucking my wife, but thanks for letting me know you find me attractive."

I'd like to kick his ass, but I can't exactly move right now. "I got the kid, didn't I?"

"Yeah, but you had a whole team behind you, Pryce. All of us could've gotten in and out without anyone getting shot, but you had to be the idiot who went in trying to prove something."

It's easy for him to say it. He came home in one piece. I didn't and I'm still trying to find out how to live the way I once did. For the most part, I don't have issues, but some days...it sucks ass.

"You know, when you're sitting over there with both legs, it's a prick thing to do to point out the errors."

"Prick thing? How about rushing into a building that hadn't been cleared or assessed? I think that's a dick move."

He's right. "I just...I felt alive again."

For the first time since my injury I was out there, doing something. No one was babying me. I was with my team, working to get the rest of our guys out of danger. In my gut, I knew they were there and the longer we waited, the more my mind ran through things I couldn't bear.

Mark's anger dissipates. Thankfully, he doesn't look at me with pity. I would have to find a way to punch him in the face.

"I get that, but what happens now? What if you lose your arm, Ben?"

"Ben?" Gretchen's soft voice says from the door.

"I'll leave you two," Mark says, looking at Gretchen. "He's a lucky guy, Jilted. A lucky man and he's a fucking idiot."

Her eyes meet mine. "I see."

"Get out, Twilight."

"Don't break the bed, Hulk."

I flip him off and she moves toward me. "Are you okay?"

"I'm fine."

She pushes her hair back, which is her nervous tell. "What happened?"

I tell her a very loose version, not wanting to freak her out. My team was exemplary, they found their target and got him out, but in the process, they were pinned down. We train to work through every possibility, and thankfully, they left the skeleton crew back to handle any mishaps. They secured the kid, got word to us, and then we went in.

The part I don't tell her is that I wasn't waiting for nightfall. I had an opportunity and I wasn't going to lose it. By doing that, I could've gotten us all killed.

Hell, if it weren't for Mark and Jackson's quick thinking, I definitely would be in a different room in the hospital right now.

"And you were shot?" The fear in her voice, the red rims around her eyes tell me everything. "You...could've died because of it? Why would you do this? Why did you? What if something else happened? What if your injuries were worse than they are?"

This shook her.

"They're not."

"God! You don't know that, Ben. You're not a doctor!"

"No, but I'm not going to fucking stand aside when others are in danger. That's not who I am!"

Gretchen wipes a tear and turns her head, trying to hide her face. "I wouldn't expect you to, but...you're hurt now."

When she finally meets my eyes...I see it. I see the look I prayed I would never see again. Her eyes are haunted by realizing I'm not what she thought. I'm not safe, secure, or able to give her the life she wants.

I'll never fit into her life list. The one she clings to.

I'll be the disappointment at the end, leaving her with more of a mess than walking away now. I have to let her go, allow her to find someone that can be the man she deserves.

She needs to learn how to be free, and I won't be the man to put her in a cage.

"This is who I'll always be, Gretchen. There's no changing me into the lawyer you loved before. I'm a fighter. I won't give up and if I die in the process—so be it. I will never give this life up."

She takes a step back. "What does that even mean?"

"It means I'm not the right guy for you. I don't want you to delude yourself that I will ever be him."

Her lips part and I hear the quick intake of breath. "I don't understand. Why are you pushing me away?"

Because I'm a coward and I can't bear the idea of hurting you later, so I'll do it now.

"I'm not. I'm just illuminating you into the reality. It's why I told you I was only *showing* you what a date was, I wasn't actually dating you. I will never be serious about a woman again, so if that's what you're looking for...move on now and save us both the wasting of time."

Her eyes narrow. "You're kidding me, right?"

My heart is breaking as I look at the hurt that flashes in her face. "No, I don't know what *you* thought we were doing. I was very clear from the beginning."

She steps forward, hands balled in fists, and I pray she hits me. Not that it would be anything like the pain I'm feeling by doing this.

"You're right, Ben. You were crystal clear. I'm so sorry for my mistake, it won't ever happen again. Feel better."

Gretchen turns, trying to hide the pain in her eyes, and walks out the door, leaving me in more pain than the bullet wound in my shoulder.

Chapter Seventeen

Gretchen

Heartbreak is such a stupid word. Hearts can't break, but they can ache. And that's what mine is doing now.

I know it's in there, still beating, because the aching that's coming from my chest has me sobbing.

Catherine drove me home without asking many questions. She just told me whatever I needed she'd be there for me—like always. I don't know that I could've said a word without breaking out in tears. I needed to stay quiet because then I could bottle it up.

Today, the bottle can no longer be contained.

I thought I had it together. I really did. But it's been two days and I can't stop the tears from falling.

"Gretchen, I'm worried." Catherine's voice is soft. "You weren't like this after..." I look up, but my eyes hurt to open. She sighs and then continues. "I'm saying that you were up, not lying in bed like a lump after your wedding was cancelled. Your *wedding*, Gretch! To a man you were supposed to spend your life with and you spend a few weeks with Ben and you're a mess."

"I'm fine," I say defiantly.

"You're not."

"Okay, I'm not, but I will be."

Even I don't believe it.

How did Ben wound me so deeply? I thought we were more. I thought he could be everything. I was so ready for a life together and now...I'm alone.

She sighs. "What happened?"

"I'm an idiot."

"Well, I don't believe that, but tell me so I can decide."

I roll over, pulling the blanket with me. "I really need to learn not to sleep with guys I work with. Shit! I'm going to be unemployed again."

I really liked this job. It was fun being around Mark, Natalie, the other SEALs and...him. There is something really unique about the way their company works and I was finally revising all their contracts to actually benefit them. Plus, there's still the whole shady lawyer who seems to have disappeared.

Now what the hell am I going to do?

"You're not going to be unemployed." Catherine rolls her eyes. "If anyone will be, it won't be you. I can assure you of that."

I don't want Ben to lose his job. He needs it much more than I do. "Don't even think about letting anyone go." I grip her hand.

"Okay. Just talk to me. I'm here and I want to help."

"And say what? Say that I was a fool who thought there was something there? I was so desperate to be loved again that I deluded myself that his fake dates were real? I wanted him so bad that I truly believed we made love. I thought each kiss was more than just him giving me a fucking gauge on what I should want from a man."

"You were fake dating? Like, it was just a show?"

"Well, *he* was! I thought...I don't know, but I was wrong."

I am really the absolute worst judge of character. I thought it was all real. Again, I fooled myself into wanting someone that didn't want me back. How stupid am I?

"I don't understand."

I tell her about his brilliant ideas and how it felt...different. "It wasn't acting, Cat. I swear, no one could act that way. He said it wasn't at one point. Maybe...maybe the first date, but even then, the way he kissed me, held me, smiled at me, there's no way that it wasn't real. He was so honest that I still can't reconcile it, you know? When it was Harold, I wasn't even half this upset. I was almost...relieved to some extent because I *knew*. I *knew* it wasn't real love. I knew that what we had was superficial at best and that I was only with him because he was my best shot at my stupid list. With Ben, he was my whole list."

"You love him."

"How?" I yell and sit up. "How can I love someone who was

so...not in love with me. How can I love someone after just a few weeks?"

Catherine shakes her head with a sad smile. "You really are an idiot."

"Gee, thanks."

"She's right," a deep voice says from the doorway. "You are an idiot, but I'm the biggest one."

There stands Ben, all six plus feet of him. His arm is in a sling, the beginnings of a beard are growing, and he has dark circles under his eyes. The hospital band is on his wrist and he's cloaked in regret.

"What are you doing here? How did you get in here?"

"I have a key," he says as he walks forward. "And as for why I'm here...well, I'm here to grovel, beg, and do anything for you to forgive me."

Catherine stands, moving to the wall. "That's my cue." I look to her, asking her with my eyes not to leave. What does the traitor do? Wink and then slink out.

"I can't talk about this," I say to him. "I can't hear any more from you."

The last time I loved someone, I hoped when they spoke, they'd fix what they'd broken. That didn't happen. Instead, I was just reassured that I was fooling myself. With Ben, I thought it was different.

I'd rather believe what we had was real than allow him to confirm it was a lie.

"Please don't..." I ask.

"Just listen," he says with pleading eyes. "I was so sure that you were going to walk away. I thought you saw me in that bed and it was the end. I spent the next four days angry at the world, the doctors, my friends, but mostly myself. It wasn't you who saw me in that bed and wanted to leave, it was me." I close my eyes, a tear leaking out as he explains. "I didn't want to fail you and have you deal with less of a man. I thought if I could let you go, then you'd be free. Free to find someone who could love you better, but..."

"But?"

Ben sits on the bed, taking my hand in his. I marvel at how well we fit together. How just a simple touch like this can make me feel like all is right in the world. The fact that his closeness allows me to breathe easier. When we were kids, it was like that.

He made everything seem just...better.

I always felt that he would do whatever he could to make me smile.

When I felt like I'd lost him again, my heart was decimated.

"But I never want to know if that's possible. I don't ever want another man to touch you, know you, because he will never love you the way I do. *I* want to be there every night, fight with you, laugh with you, take you on a million dates, be the man that you see me as and continue to prove I can be that."

I shake my head and then touch his face with my hand. "You are that man."

"No. I'm not yet, but I plan to be...for you."

He is more of that man than anyone I've ever met. He came here, apparently straight from the hospital, to tell me he was wrong.

"I don't know what to say," I confess.

"Say you'll forgive me for being an asshole. Tell me that there's still a chance."

I look up into his chocolate brown eyes, knowing I never want to look at another's. "I don't think I could resist you if I tried. Just don't ever push me away like that."

"I won't."

"I'll always be honest. If something is too much, I'll tell you."

This is the one lesson I've learned. I can't control the things around me, but I can control how I deal with them. Being honest is necessary. I used to let things get to be too much and then the issue was so much bigger than it had to be.

"And I will trust that what you say is true."

I bring my lips to his. "We have a lot of trust issues between us. People who were supposed to love us have hurt us, but we don't have to hurt each other. I don't want the sins of our past to dictate our futures."

He nods. "Is that what you want?"

"What?"

"A future."

"With you?"

Ben pushes my hair back, holding my face. "With me."

I close my eyes, resting my head against his. "Forever. You've always been my forever."

And then, we don't say anything else. Because we're much too busy to speak.

Epilogue

Gretchen

~Three Years Later~

"Where is he?" I ask as I pace the bridal suite. If this happens to me again, I will lose my ever-loving mind.

"He'll be here," Catherine says and then glances at Ashton before smiling at me.

Ashton rubs her small baby bump and grumbles, "If he's not, I'll kill him. Doesn't he care I'm stuffed in this dress that I've let out three times?"

"Yes, I'm sure you're what he's worried about," I huff.

No one told her to get knocked up.

"Relax, both of you. Ben will not stand Gretchen up." Cat tries to be the voice of reason. "He loves her too much."

My phone rings and déjà vu hits me like a ton of bricks. Panic builds as I rush over to it.

"Ben?"

"Babe. There was a major accident on 264 and we're totally stuck, but I called Mark and he's on his way with his motorcycle to get me and Jackson."

"You're not standing me up?" I ask with fear in my voice.

"Never. I have been waiting for this day for freaking years. Just know I'm coming for you."

I smile, clutching my hand to my chest. "Okay. Just hurry."

"I'm trying."

"I know."

Ben clears his throat. "I love you."

"I love you, too."

I hang up and walk over to the window. It's such a gorgeous day and we found the cutest church right off the beach. At first, we thought we'd do a beach wedding, save the fanfare and all, but my mother wasn't having it.

The Catholic guilt is strong with that one.

She pretty much demanded that we'd be married in a church, surrounded by family.

Which is now a wedding of over three hundred people.

Between my family and Ben's family, which means everyone he ever served with, our intimate wedding is now a shit-show.

"Where is he?" My mother opens the door, and I can see the worry on her face.

"He'll be here, Mrs. Burke," Ashton says. "Or he'll have to deal with my pregnant ass."

"Ashton Caputo, you watch your mouth in church."

My mother will forever be trying to reform her. I figured by now she'd have tired of it, but it seems she just becomes more determined with each of the sins Ashton commits.

"You can't save me, Mama B."

"No one can save her. The sooner we accept this, the happier we'll be." I try to get my mother's attention or these two will go toe to toe and my mother loses to no one. "Ben is stuck in traffic but Mark went to get him on the motorcycle."

She nods once. "Okay, otherwise I couldn't be responsible for what your Uncle Tony and father do. Lord knows we had to convince Tony that you actually called the wedding off so he didn't..."

Ashton laughs. "Have Harold swim with the fishes?"

My mother tries to look affronted but she fails.

"He did like to scuba dive. He might have liked it," I explain with a giggle.

"Gretchen!" Mother chastises me. "Not in church."

"I think the Lord would understand," Catherine tosses in.

The four of us burst out into a fit of laughter. My mother fusses over my dress and then moves on to the girls. They're like my sisters and no one is exempt in this group.

After a few minutes, she goes out to assure the crowd the wedding is in fact happening. More like assuring my father who has spent a boat load giving me the wedding of my mother's dreams.

A knock comes at the door and Mark peeks his head in. "I got your groom."

"Good, now we can get her hitched and I can get this dress off," Ashton says.

"Thanks, Mark."

He winks. "Anything for you, Jilted."

I flip him off.

Daddy enters with a smile. "You ready?"

"I am."

Catherine and Ashton each kiss my cheek as they start to walk out. I am so glad they're by my side. I couldn't have done this—for the second time—without them.

"He's a good man," Dad says as he makes his way to me.

"I know."

"Came right to me, shook my hand, apologized and explained. He left that limo on the interstate to get here. Not like the last idiot."

I smile, loving that my Dad likes Ben. They've bonded a lot over the last few years, but then again, Ben has made every effort to show them he's different.

We go up to New Jersey for the holidays, and it also doesn't hurt that he's a die-hard Giants fan, which makes him an automatic win to Daddy. More than that, I know it's how he treats me. My father has always wanted me to find someone to love me like he loves my mother. They met very similarly to us. They were high school sweethearts that got married right out of school. No one thought they'd last, but here they are, still ridiculously in love.

"Are you ready to give me away, Daddy?"

He kisses my forehead. "No, but I'm ready to give you to a worthy man."

I hook my hand in his arm, leaning on him for support. My stomach is in knots as we make our way down the hall toward the aisle. When we get there, the music changes and I focus on my breathing.

I'm so ready for this. Ready to be Mrs. Benjamin Pryce.

When we get to our spot, I see him for the first time.

I promised myself I wouldn't cry, but the look on his face makes it impossible.

My father starts to walk and tears fall with each step. They're not sad tears though, it's joy. I've never been happier than I am right now.

Ben looks at me like I'm the center of the world and he's my anchor. Together, we ground each other.

When I get to where he stands, I see the unshed tears in his eyes.

My father places my hand in his and kisses my cheek.

"I'm sorry I was late," Ben says softly.

"I'm just glad you made it."

"It would've taken an army to keep me from you."

I smile, wishing I could kiss him right now, but I know it has to wait.

The priest begins, calling our attention away from our private conversation.

Through each part of the ceremony I think about how we got here. The struggles and triumphs that lead us to this moment. We've had no shortage of issues, from his recovery after being shot to me adjusting to not being a practicing lawyer and feeling a little out of place. Both of us have been each other's rock and I know that no matter what we face, we'll come out on top.

We say our vows, the same that many long-lasting couples have promised each other, but add our own touch to assure each other of what we both need.

"I, Gretchen Burke, promise to always be there, even when you think I won't be. I promise to give you my heart, my love, and my soul without question. You will never have to wonder because I won't give you cause to doubt me. From this point forward, trust me to never fail you and always come from a place of love. Even if I'm angry, tired, or just in a mood, know that the constant will be how much you mean to me. Know that you're my heart, Ben. Always."

Ben's eyes are locked on mine as he speaks. "I, Benjamin Pryce, promise to love, honor, and cherish you. I think I've been waiting to say those words since I was thirteen, because that's the first time I felt love. You didn't know it, I didn't even really understand it, but I've loved you since the beginning. I promise to be the man you deserve and when I'm not, I will do whatever I can to fix my shortcomings. I vow that my love will be the constant you can always rely on...forevermore."

And that last word says it all.

Forevermore.

He looks to the priest, who gives a nod. "I now pronounce you husband and wife. You may—"

He doesn't get to finish because Ben already has me in his arms. I grip his shoulders as he seals our union with a breathtaking kiss.

Thank you for reading Ben & Gretchen's story. If you loved this group of guys, then be sure to check out Beloved and fall for all the Salvation Series heroes.

If you'd like a get an EXCLUSIVE look at what I have coming next, sign up!

* * * *

Also from 1001 Dark Nights and Corinne Michaels, discover Say You Won't Let Go.

Sign up for the 1001 Dark Nights Newsletter
and be entered to win a Tiffany Key necklace.

There's a contest every month!

Go to www.1001DarkNights.com to subscribe.

As a bonus, all subscribers can download
FIVE FREE exclusive books!

Discover 1001 Dark Nights Collection Six

DRAGON CLAIMED by Donna Grant
A Dark Kings Novella

ASHES TO INK by Carrie Ann Ryan
A Montgomery Ink: Colorado Springs Novella

ENSNARED by Elisabeth Naughton
An Eternal Guardians Novella

EVERMORE by Corinne Michaels
A Salvation Series Novella

VENGEANCE by Rebecca Zanetti
A Dark Protectors/Rebels Novella

ELI'S TRIUMPH by Joanna Wylde
A Reapers MC Novella

CIPHER by Larissa Ione
A Demonica Underworld Novella

RESCUING MACIE by Susan Stoker
A Delta Force Heroes Novella

ENCHANTED by Lexi Blake
A Masters and Mercenaries Novella

TAKE THE BRIDE by Carly Phillips
A Knight Brothers Novella

INDULGE ME by J. Kenner
A Stark Ever After Novella

THE KING by Jennifer L. Armentrout
A Wicked Novella

QUIET MAN by Kristen Ashley
A Dream Man Novella

ABANDON by Rachel Van Dyken
A Seaside Pictures Novella

THE OPEN DOOR by Laurelin Paige
A Found Duet Novella

CLOSER by Kylie Scott
A Stage Dive Novella

SOMETHING JUST LIKE THIS by Jennifer Probst
A Stay Novella

BLOOD NIGHT by Heather Graham
A Krewe of Hunters Novella

TWIST OF FATE by Jill Shalvis
A Heartbreaker Bay Novella

MORE THAN PLEASURE YOU by Shayla Black
A More Than Words Novella

WONDER WITH ME by Kristen Proby
A With Me In Seattle Novella

THE DARKEST ASSASSIN by Gena Showalter
A Lords of the Underworld Novella

Also from 1001 Dark Nights:
DAMIEN by J. Kenner

Discover 1001 Dark Nights

COLLECTION ONE
FOREVER WICKED by Shayla Black
CRIMSON TWILIGHT by Heather Graham
CAPTURED IN SURRENDER by Liliana Hart
SILENT BITE: A SCANGUARDS WEDDING by Tina Folsom
DUNGEON GAMES by Lexi Blake
AZAGOTH by Larissa Ione
NEED YOU NOW by Lisa Renee Jones
SHOW ME, BABY by Cherise Sinclair
ROPED IN by Lorelei James
TEMPTED BY MIDNIGHT by Lara Adrian
THE FLAME by Christopher Rice
CARESS OF DARKNESS by Julie Kenner

COLLECTION TWO
WICKED WOLF by Carrie Ann Ryan
WHEN IRISH EYES ARE HAUNTING by Heather Graham
EASY WITH YOU by Kristen Proby
MASTER OF FREEDOM by Cherise Sinclair
CARESS OF PLEASURE by Julie Kenner
ADORED by Lexi Blake
HADES by Larissa Ione
RAVAGED by Elisabeth Naughton
DREAM OF YOU by Jennifer L. Armentrout
STRIPPED DOWN by Lorelei James
RAGE/KILLIAN by Alexandra Ivy/Laura Wright
DRAGON KING by Donna Grant
PURE WICKED by Shayla Black
HARD AS STEEL by Laura Kaye
STROKE OF MIDNIGHT by Lara Adrian
ALL HALLOWS EVE by Heather Graham
KISS THE FLAME by Christopher Rice
DARING HER LOVE by Melissa Foster
TEASED by Rebecca Zanetti
THE PROMISE OF SURRENDER by Liliana Hart

COLLECTION THREE
HIDDEN INK by Carrie Ann Ryan
BLOOD ON THE BAYOU by Heather Graham
SEARCHING FOR MINE by Jennifer Probst
DANCE OF DESIRE by Christopher Rice
ROUGH RHYTHM by Tessa Bailey
DEVOTED by Lexi Blake
Z by Larissa Ione
FALLING UNDER YOU by Laurelin Paige
EASY FOR KEEPS by Kristen Proby
UNCHAINED by Elisabeth Naughton
HARD TO SERVE by Laura Kaye
DRAGON FEVER by Donna Grant
KAYDEN/SIMON by Alexandra Ivy/Laura Wright
STRUNG UP by Lorelei James
MIDNIGHT UNTAMED by Lara Adrian
TRICKED by Rebecca Zanetti
DIRTY WICKED by Shayla Black
THE ONLY ONE by Lauren Blakely
SWEET SURRENDER by Liliana Hart

COLLECTION FOUR
ROCK CHICK REAWAKENING by Kristen Ashley
ADORING INK by Carrie Ann Ryan
SWEET RIVALRY by K. Bromberg
SHADE'S LADY by Joanna Wylde
RAZR by Larissa Ione
ARRANGED by Lexi Blake
TANGLED by Rebecca Zanetti
HOLD ME by J. Kenner
SOMEHOW, SOME WAY by Jennifer Probst
TOO CLOSE TO CALL by Tessa Bailey
HUNTED by Elisabeth Naughton
EYES ON YOU by Laura Kaye
BLADE by Alexandra Ivy/Laura Wright
DRAGON BURN by Donna Grant
TRIPPED OUT by Lorelei James
STUD FINDER by Lauren Blakely

MIDNIGHT UNLEASHED by Lara Adrian
HALLOW BE THE HAUNT by Heather Graham
DIRTY FILTHY FIX by Laurelin Paige
THE BED MATE by Kendall Ryan
NIGHT GAMES by CD Reiss
NO RESERVATIONS by Kristen Proby
DAWN OF SURRENDER by Liliana Hart

COLLECTION FIVE
BLAZE ERUPTING by Rebecca Zanetti
ROUGH RIDE by Kristen Ashley
HAWKYN by Larissa Ione
RIDE DIRTY by Laura Kaye
ROME'S CHANCE by Joanna Wylde
THE MARRIAGE ARRANGEMENT by Jennifer Probst
SURRENDER by Elisabeth Naughton
INKED NIGHTS by Carrie Ann Ryan
ENVY by Rachel Van Dyken
PROTECTED by Lexi Blake
THE PRINCE by Jennifer L. Armentrout
PLEASE ME by J. Kenner
WOUND TIGHT by Lorelei James
STRONG by Kylie Scott
DRAGON NIGHT by Donna Grant
TEMPTING BROOKE by Kristen Proby
HAUNTED BE THE HOLIDAYS by Heather Graham
CONTROL by K. Bromberg
HUNKY HEARTBREAKER by Kendall Ryan
THE DARKEST CAPTIVE by Gena Showalter

Also from 1001 Dark Nights:

TAME ME by J. Kenner
THE SURRENDER GATE By Christopher Rice
SERVICING THE TARGET By Cherise Sinclair
TEMPT ME by J. Kenner

About Corinne Michaels

New York Times, USA Today, and Wall Street Journal Bestseller Corinne Michaels is the author of multiple romance novels. She's an emotional, witty, sarcastic, and fun-loving mom of two beautiful children. Corinne is happily married to the man of her dreams and is a former Navy wife.

After spending months away from her husband while he was deployed, reading and writing was her escape from the loneliness. She enjoys putting her characters through intense heartbreak and finding a way to heal them through their struggles. Her stories are chock full of emotion, humor, and unrelenting love.

Discover More Corinne Michaels

Say You Won't Let Go: A Return to Me/Masters and Mercenaries Novella
by Corinne Michaels

I've had two goals my entire life:
1. Make it big in country music.
2. Get the hell out of Bell Buckle.

I was doing it. I was on my way, until Cooper Townsend landed backstage at my show in Dallas.

This gorgeous, rugged, man of few words was one cowboy I couldn't afford to let distract me. But with his slow smile and rough hands, I just couldn't keep away.

Now, there are outside forces conspiring against us. Maybe we should've known better? Maybe not. Even with the protection from Wade Rycroft, bodyguard for McKay-Taggart, I still don't feel safe. I won't let him get hurt because of me. All I know is that I want to hold on, but know the right thing to do is to let go…

Beloved
Salvation Book 1
By Corinne Michaels
Now Available

Men suck.

They break you. Leave you. Take everything until there's nothing left. And frankly, I'm done allowing them to make me feel insignificant. So, forget men. I'll just throw myself into my job, because at least that never fails me.

Jackson has other plans, though. I refuse to be impressed by his perfect body, the cute dimple on his cheek, or the rugged stubble on his face. Jackson Cole can be resisted.

But, I'm only fooling myself.

He's going to wear me down. I can feel it. In the end he'll prove that once again, I'm no one's beloved.

* * * *

Prologue

To belong to someone.
All I've ever wanted is to be loved. I crave it—need it, desire it—more than food and water. I long for undying love and affection. The kind of love that bonds souls. The kind of love that's so deep two become one.
To be someone's beloved.
As a child I had my father, who adored and worshipped me—I was his perfect little daughter. He held me when I was sad, kissed my knee when I fell and got hurt, and read me bedtime stories. I was his princess, his daughter, his entire world.
What happens to a little girl when all of that stops? When she's no longer her father's perfect angel, but *instead* a painful reminder of his past. What happens to her when he pushes her aside and shows her he

doesn't want her anymore?

"*I just can't stay, Catherine. It hurts too much.*" *His eyes are filled with pain and regret.*

"*Daddy, I love you! Please don't go. I won't cry anymore. I'll be good,*" *I plead as I look into the dark brown eyes that mirror mine. My heart is begging for understanding from all this confusion and change. It's my ninth birthday, we finished cake and presents, and he's leaving. If only I could go back in time and change my wish. I'd forget about the silly bike and wish for him to stay.*

"*It's not you, baby girl. You have to understand—it's too much. Your mom and I don't love each other anymore.*" *He looks into my eyes, unwavering, as I continue to plead.*

"*Don't you love me, Daddy?*" *I ask the man who is supposed to love me forever, the man who's supposed to never leave me.*

"*I do, but I have to go now. You be good. Good-bye, Catherine.*" *He kisses the top of my head and I grab onto his leg for dear life. I know, even at this age, this will be the last time I see my father.*

He pries me off his leg and turns without another word. And I watch the man who promised to always be there leave me behind without another glance.

He broke me.

He ruined me.

And he won't be the last man to do so.

* * * *

CHAPTER 1

"Ashton, I'm running over to Neil's house. I'll be back in a bit!"

Our wedding invitations arrived. They're beautiful, everything I could've hoped for. I can't wait to show him. Not that he's really into the details, but we spent a lot of time choosing these. It'll be such a relief when we finally move in together and stop all this back and forth. Ashton and I signed our lease a month before Neil proposed, so I couldn't leave and screw her out of half the rent. Though I adore my best friend, I would've loved to have lived with Neil as we planned the wedding. Thankfully, the big day is in four months and we'll finally be under one roof. I'm excited and anxious to make everything official.

"Okay. I'll be here," she says, walking toward me.

"Don't get into any trouble while I'm gone." I wink as I grab my purse and rush out the door. Once I get in the car I send him a quick text.

Me: On my way. I have a surprise!

Ten minutes later, I'm pulling into a parking space in front of his cozy two-bedroom townhome in the trendy section of Hoboken. This area is all older homes on cobblestone streets. It's a place I look forward to building a life and starting a family in. I gather my purse and the invitations and hop out, excited to share this piece of our future with him. His car is in the driveway, but the door is locked. Digging for my keys, my bag topples over, spilling all my belongings on the stairs. After collecting everything, I use my key to get into his house.

As the door opens I hear a low moan. Slowly I lift my eyes. Nothing could've prepared me for the sight before me. I freeze, watching my worst nightmare unfold.

The shock ripples through me, coming in waves of horror and pain.

And no matter how much I want to … I can't look away.

The man I love, the man I'm going to marry, is having sex with one of my friends.

Neil has Piper bent over on the couch—the couch *I* picked out—and is taking her from behind. His head is turned toward the door, his eyes are closed, and his face is pure ecstasy as he drives into her, enjoying every second of it while my world crumbles. With each thrust I feel the floor falling out from under me. I can hear them, see them, smell the sex in the air. Each slap of skin on skin, each grunt and moan tears through me like a knife slicing my veins open. I'm bleeding out, and there's no stopping it.

I close my eyes, begging for this not to be real, hoping this is a sick joke or a bad dream, praying that when I open them again, this cruel vision will fade away. When I gather the strength to look at them, I realize this isn't a joke or a dream—it's reality.

Piper's head is thrown back as she moans. "More. Harder!"

His hands grip her hips as he rears back and rams into her.

"Neil, yes!" Her loud, high-pitched voice screams out, "Oh! I'm coming. Oh. My. God. Neil! Fuck!"

Unable to control the shaking of my hands, the invitations fall to the floor. My sob breaks through the sounds of their pleasure, alerting them to my presence. The air punches through me as both their heads snap up and Neil's eyes lock on mine.

"Catherine." He stops moving, staring at me with wide eyes. "I can explain."

He grabs the blanket off the back of the couch and covers himself, hastily throwing another one at Piper.

"Explain? You can't fucking explain!" I choke out as the tears begin to flood my vision. "Oh my God! You … you …"

My limbs are tingling and my breathing is shallow as I try to remain standing. Everything around me is fading, but cruelly, my mind keeps the two people in front of me crystal clear. I close my eyes, hoping to give myself a reprieve.

Neil speaks as I grip the doorway for support. "Give me a minute and we can talk."

I don't want to talk. I want to pour bleach in my eyes and rip out my heart so it will stop hurting so much. Nothing he can say will erase this. Ever. My heart will never be the same. Cheating is bad enough, but for me to witness it—with one of my friends, no less—is torture.

On behalf of 1001 Dark Nights,

Liz Berry and M.J. Rose would like to thank ~

Steve Berry
Doug Scofield
Kim Guidroz
Jillian Stein
InkSlinger PR
Dan Slater
Asha Hossain
Chris Graham
Fedora Chen
Kasi Alexander
Jessica Johns
Dylan Stockton
Richard Blake
and Simon Lipskar